"If you're in troub[le]
Pierce said.

Grace took a deep breath and pulled one of her rehearsed stories from her repertoire. "If you must know, I didn't lose my job. I had a bad breakup with an ex. I took all of his possessions he'd left at my place and dumped them. I decided to take a short vacation while he cools down."

"Remind me not to make you mad."

He reached over and took both her hands in his. The touch sent her emotions on a dangerous spiral. She couldn't give in to the desire that sparked inside her. A relationship with Pierce had nowhere to go. It would cause her to make bad decisions.

Pierce placed a thumb under her chin and tilted her face until his lips were only a hairbreadth away. "I want you to stay, Grace, because I really like having you here."

His lips touched hers. A longing struck full force, a need so intense she had to struggle to breathe.

RIDING SHOTGUN

JOANNA WAYNE

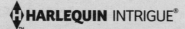

To all my readers who love a good family story
with a fairy-tale ending. A special thanks to my own
wonderful family, who make my life so special,
and to my fantastic editor, who has made
my last twenty years of writing a joy.

ISBN-13: 978-1-335-72071-9

Riding Shotgun

Copyright © 2016 by Jo Ann Vest

Recycling programs
for this product may
not exist in your area.

This edition published by arrangement with Harlequin Books S.A.

For questions and comments about the quality of this book, please contact us at CustomerService@Harlequin.com.

Printed in U.S.A.

www.Harlequin.com

Joanna Wayne began her professional writing career in 1994. Now, more than fifty published books later, Joanna has gained a worldwide following with her cutting-edge romantic suspense and Texas family series, such as Sons of Troy Ledger and Big "D" Dads. Joanna currently resides in a small community north of Houston, Texas, with her husband. You may write Joanna at PO Box 852, Montgomery, TX 77356, or connect with her at joannawayne.com.

Books by Joanna Wayne

Harlequin Intrigue

The Kavanaughs

Riding Shotgun

Big "D" Dads: The Daltons

Trumped Up Charges
Unrepentant Cowboy
Hard Ride to Dry Gulch
Midnight Rider
Showdown at Shadow Junction
Ambush at Dry Gulch

Sons of Troy Ledger

Cowboy Swagger
Genuine Cowboy
AK-Cowboy
Cowboy Fever
Cowboy Conspiracy

Big "D" Dads

Son of a Gun
Live Ammo
Big Shot

Visit the Author Profile page at Harlequin.com for more titles.

CAST OF CHARACTERS

Grace Addison—At twenty-four, she is running scared, living a nightmare that she is sure will never end.

Pierce Lawrence—Former navy SEAL, a hero in every sense of the word.

Jaci Lawrence—Pierce's daughter.

Charlie and Esther Kavanaugh—The couple who took Pierce and his two younger brothers in after the death of their parents.

Riley and Tucker Lawrence—Pierce's younger brothers.

Sheriff Cavazos—The local sheriff.

Andy Malone—Former SEAL buddy of Pierce who is now with the FBI.

Buck Stalling—Part-time wrangler at the Double K Ranch.

Dudley Miles—Imprisoned now but was the best friend of Charlie Kavanaugh.

Reid Peterson—A member of a drug gang in San Antonio.

Tom Lacoste—Grace's ex-husband.

Prologue

Esther Kavanaugh lifted the lid and sniffed the aroma of pinto beans, spices and the hunk of pork she'd added for flavor. Probably too much salt and fat for their health, but it was just the way Charlie liked it. Fifty-three years of eating her cooking and he still bragged that she was the best cook in Texas.

She grabbed her oversize metal spoon and gave the beans a final stir before cutting off the gas. Beans were ready. So were the turnip greens and corn bread. Fresh onion was sliced. She didn't need the clock to tell her it was lunchtime. Her stomach was doing that for her.

Still, she glanced up and checked the hands on the loud ticking metal clock hanging on the opposite wall. Ten after twelve, which meant it was pushing twelve thirty. Old clock always ran slow, but it was close enough for Esther. At seventy-two, she was starting to run a bit slow herself these days.

Charlie had never worried much with punctuality, though he was up with the sun each morning.

Claimed his cows didn't watch the clock, so why should he.

He was seldom late for lunch, though. Must be trying to finish up some chore, probably working on that old tractor of his. She tried to get him to replace it, but he wouldn't hear of it. Never throw away what can be fixed, he insisted.

She filled two glasses with ice and poured one to the top with fresh brewed sweet tea. She took her drink to the back porch to wait for Charlie. Mid-September but the sun was blazing down like August, making the humid air practically steamy.

Settling in the wooden rocker, she let her thoughts drift to the past. That was another thing about getting older, not that seventy-two was all that old, but she did find herself thinking backward more and more these days.

Like the first time she'd seen Charlie come hurtling through the gate at their small-town rodeo on the back of a snorting, kicking giant of a bull. He hadn't lasted the required eight seconds. Hadn't even lasted two.

But when he'd gotten up, dusted off his jeans, looked right at her and tipped his hat, she was a goner. She'd loved that man every day since.

She sipped her tea and rocked.

Thirty minutes later, her glass was empty except for small chunks of melting ice. Where in the world was that old man of hers? It wasn't like Charlie to be this late when he knew food was waiting. She went back inside, picked up the house phone and called his cell number.

No answer. She called again. And again.

Finally, she left a message urging him to call her back. No use to panic, she reminded herself as her nerves grew edgier. His hearing wasn't that great anymore and he was too damned stubborn to admit he needed hearing aids. He probably couldn't hear the phone over the equipment he was operating.

No doubt he'd be calling her back any moment. After all, the only reason he'd agreed to carry what he called the most annoying invention of all time was in case she had an emergency and needed him.

Ten minutes later, he hadn't called back. Her stomach churned, though she'd lost her appetite.

She'd best go check on Charlie. She took off down the worn path, past the chicken coop and to the barn. The tractor was in plain sight. Charlie wasn't. She was almost running by the time she neared the open barn door.

She stopped stock-still. A stream of crimson snaked out of the barn and spread over the dirt. She went numb, struck with sudden, paralyzing fear.

Then, heart pounding, she grabbed her chest and stumbled inside.

A pool of blood. A head split wide-open. A gun.

The images ripped through her. Icy fingers wrapped around her heart, squeezing so hard that her chest seemed to explode. The last thing she remembered was the metallic taste on her tongue as she collapsed face-first into the river of Charlie's blood.

Chapter One

Three months later

Grace Cotton looked up and into a pair of twinkling gray-blue eyes encircled by deep wrinkles and saggy skin. Elizabeth Howe was just one of the many reasons she loved working in the small-town Tennessee library.

"You're all set," Grace said. "As soon as the book is available, I'll give you a call."

"Tell them not to dally too long. At ninety-two, I don't have time to wait around on a novel. I don't even buy green bananas."

Grace smiled at the joke even though Mrs. Howe repeated it every time she visited the library. Still, the feisty woman was amazing for her age. Got around just fine with the help of a jeweled, engraved cane, a gift to her from an English duke she'd met on a cruise aboard the *Queen Mary* a few years back. She'd obviously enchanted him the way she did everyone who knew her.

"Buy all the green bananas you want," Grace teased. "I expect you'll still be devouring romance novels long after I've retired."

"No chance of that, but I'll be reading them as long as I can. Even old worn-out bodies like mine need a little fantasy."

Young bodies, too, though Grace steered clear of it. Longing bred temptation, and she didn't dare so much as flirt with temptation.

"Bundle up before you go outside," Grace reminded her. "That north wind cuts to the bone."

"Don't I know it," Elizabeth said, pulling her parka tight over her slender body. She zipped it and tugged the hood over short silver wisps of her hair until she was just a wrinkled face peeking out of a furry frame.

She reached for the books she'd chosen from the shelves, several Grace knew she'd read before.

"Let me help you get those to the car," Grace offered.

Elizabeth waved her off. "I don't need help. I'm parked under the overhang in the book drop-off lane. Right by the no-parking sign." She winked. "I figure having a great-grandson who's a deputy ought to get me a perk on a day like this."

"I'd say you're right." Not that anyone in town would question where Elizabeth parked her fifteen-year-old blue Honda. She was a living legend in this mountain town where she'd been born and lived all her life.

Grace envied her that. Having so many close

friends, living in one place so long she was part of the town's fabric.

Elizabeth picked up her books with her left hand and took her cane in her right. Grace would at least open the heavy front door for her. As Grace stepped from behind the counter, the door swung open, ushering in an icy blast.

Grace turned to see who else had ventured out on this cold December afternoon. The library was practically deserted today.

The young man was in jeans, an unzipped black leather jacket and no hat, clearly paying little heed to the area's first real taste of winter.

He held the door for Elizabeth and then stepped inside. His earth-colored eyes fastened on Grace, his gaze searing into hers. The intensity rattled her. She stared back.

She'd looked into those eyes before. Three days ago in the cereal aisle of Tatum's grocery. She'd looked up as she dropped a package of granola into her cart and spotted the man a few feet away, his stare as penetrating as it was now.

She'd seen him again yesterday, practically running into him on the sidewalk when she'd walked out of the town's pharmacy. Again he had stared before disappearing into the shop himself.

Panic knotted her stomach. Her fingers tightened around the corner of the counter. She took a deep breath and struggled to separate her fears from reality.

This was a small town. Running into him didn't

mean the stranger was following her. But it didn't guarantee that he wasn't, either.

He let his gaze drop from hers and glanced around the library.

"May I help you?" she asked as he approached the counter.

"I'm new in town. What do I do to get a library card?"

"You'll need a photo ID and a local address."

"No problem." He pulled out his wallet and flashed a Louisiana driver's license. A new wave of panic hit. She forced her hands not to shake as she pulled a printed form from the niche below the counter.

"Just fill this out, read the requirements for checking out books and sign your consent," she said.

"How long before I get the card?"

"I can give you a number that will allow you to check out books today. The permanent card will be mailed to your local home address."

"That'll work."

"What brings you to our area?" she asked.

"A job."

He didn't offer more. She tensed again. The small town of Mountain Edge was not a mecca for employment opportunities.

He looked over the form and then took a pen from the black plastic cup. Before making a mark, he shook his head and returned the pen to its holder. "Sorry. My phone always interrupts at the most inconvenient times."

She hadn't heard it ring. Either he had it on vibrate as the note on the counter requested or he was stalling.

He pulled his phone from his pocket as he stepped away from the counter and then walked back to the deserted reference section.

"This is it for today."

Grace startled, then turned as John Everly, a local retired attorney, set a stack of books on the counter.

She glanced at the books he'd chosen, a mix of thrillers, political intrigue and history. "Nice choices."

"Hope so. Looks like we're going to have a few more days of arctic blasts, so figured I better stock up on reading material."

"You're right," she agreed, "nothing better than getting lost in an engrossing novel while cuddled in front of a roaring fire in this type of weather."

"And it's only mid-December," he said. "I hate to think what January's going to bring."

She checked out the books and pushed them back to him. "Stay warm."

"You, too."

As he walked away, she scanned the room until she spotted the suspicious stranger near the end of one of the stacks, phone in hand, but not held to his ear. He was taking her picture.

When he saw her looking back, he quickly shoved the phone in his jacket pocket.

He knew who she was. Why else would he be taking her picture?

She fought the urge to jump across the counter and bolt for the door. But panic could lead to bad decisions. Forcing herself to stay in control, she considered her options.

But there was really only one. She'd run again, blindly, like a fox fleeing a team of vicious hunting dogs. She'd have to change her appearance, might even try out that horrible wig she'd purchased online from a costume website. She looked at least forty in that. She'd swap her contact lens for some big-rimmed glasses.

She'd find a new identity, a new job, a new town. She'd start over once again, always living on the precipice of fear and ready to run on a minute's notice.

Chapter Two

The wheels hit the runway with a thump and then bumped along a few yards before steadying. Back in the United States. Home again. For the first time in over a year.

But home to what?

A divorce from a wife who'd grown so emotionally distant that they'd stopped communicating altogether except for things concerning their daughter, Jaci.

No job prospects. No plans. And no more ties to the navy SEALs and the sense of purpose and comradery that had been his life for the past eight years.

The plane pulled up to the Jetway and jerked to a stop.

"Please remain seated until the captain turns off the seat-belt sign."

No one did, including Pierce Lawrence. He opened the overhead storage compartment and retrieved his duffel and the one of the middle-aged woman who'd had the seat next to him. They'd barely exchanged a hello on the long flight. She'd slept. He'd struggled through silent rehearsals for what he was about to face.

As wary as if he were preparing for enemy fire, he followed the crowd of passengers to baggage claim.

He spotted Leslie before she saw him. Her long blond hair fell into curls that cascaded about her narrow shoulders. Her body was as spectacular as it had been when they'd met six years ago. She wore knee-high boots, a pale blue sweater and a short fitted skirt.

He slowed and stared, half expecting a jolt of desire to take his breath away. All he felt was a foreboding sense of loss for what they'd never really had.

His gaze fell to the five-year-old girl holding tight to her hand. Jaci shifted from foot to foot expectantly, or perhaps just impatiently. Her hair was red like his mother's had been, curly like Leslie's.

His daughter looked his way but made no sign that she recognized him. The jolt hit him then. Hard, as if someone had sucker punched him in the gut.

His daughter. The reason he was back in Chicago. The reason he'd turned his back on the lifestyle he'd loved. Yet he didn't really know her and she certainly didn't know him.

It was too late to save his marriage, but he was a dad and smart enough to know that if he didn't bond with Jaci now, he might lose her forever. She'd be swallowed up by the new life Leslie would make for the two of them.

He hurried to where Leslie and Jaci were waiting. He dropped his duffel to the floor by his feet. Leslie managed a smile and slipped into his arms. Her hug lacked warmth. When he tried to kiss her, she dodged it, offering her cheek in place of her lips.

What did he expect? Their divorce would be final tomorrow.

"How was the flight?" Leslie asked.

"Long." He bent to pick up his daughter.

Jaci scooted away from him, trying to hide behind her mother's shapely legs.

"Say hello to your father, Jaci. He's come a long way to see you."

Jaci shook her head.

"That's okay," he said, though it hurt like hell. "I'm not going anywhere. We'll have plenty of time to get reacquainted."

"Yes," Leslie said. "If all goes well, the two of you will be spending a lot of time together."

Not exactly sure what that meant, he decided to let it ride. "I'll grab the rest of my luggage from baggage claim, and then let's get out of here. Maybe grab something to eat. I'm starved for some real food."

"We can have lunch at the apartment," Leslie said. "We need to talk."

They needed to talk and get this divorce and the child custody situation over and done with. Couldn't say it much plainer than that. This was definitely not the homecoming any serviceman dreamed about.

Talk during the drive to her apartment was all about Jaci, who sat in the backseat playing on an iPad.

She shrugged or totally ignored his attempts to make conversation with her.

The apartment was in a luxury complex, gated, with gardens at the entrance and a man-made brook meandering through the three-story, balconied structures. Leslie hadn't mentioned a raise or a promotion, but she'd upgraded significantly from the apartment they'd rented together when he'd last been home on leave. She clearly wasn't living like this on his military salary.

She parked next to the curb. He followed her and Jaci up the path to the front door. Jaci's hand was securely encased in her mother's as if she needed protection from the stranger referred to as her father.

He was a stranger. That was the problem. A stranger to Leslie, too. A stranger to this life that seemed positively foreign to the secret mission he'd been on in the Middle East for the past nine months.

"Nice digs," he said as he followed Leslie through the door.

"We needed more space," she said as if that explained it all. "Jaci, why don't you show your father your room and some of your favorite toys while I put lunch on the table."

Jaci looked as if she'd been asked to pick up a slimy fish with her bare hands. Pierce had a handful of medals that claimed he was brave and tough, yet facing Jaci alone daunted him.

"I can help you in the kitchen first if you'd like," he offered.

"No help needed. All I have to do is toss a salad. Everything else I picked up at the deli earlier. I thought it would be easier to talk here than at a noisy restaurant."

"No doubt."

Jaci left the kitchen and he followed her to her room. It was even more daunting than Jaci. Pink satin and lace everywhere from the curtains to the bed with its multitude of throw pillows. Looked like it had come straight from a designer's showroom. He wouldn't have dared sit on the bed and put a wrinkle in the frilly coverlet.

He wondered if Jaci did.

Not a toy out of place. Books in perfect order along a low bookshelf. Dolls on display.

"It's a very pretty room," Pierce offered.

"It's okay, I guess."

"You don't like it?"

"I wanted a cowboy coverlet like my friend Joey has, but Mommy said no."

"So, you like cowboys?" Maybe they did have some common ground. He'd loved the cowboy lifestyle himself once, had been sure he'd own his own ranch one day.

"I like horses," Jaci said.

"Have you ever ridden one?"

"Once. At Joey's birthday party, but they just walked around real slow in a circle. And they were all tied together. I don't think they liked it."

"I'm guessing they didn't," Pierce agreed. "I'll take you riding on a real horse."

Jaci tilted her head and cut her eyes at him. "Mommy says they're dangerous."

"For Mommy, maybe. But I've ridden lots of horses. I can keep you safe."

Here he was, back in her life less than an hour and already usurping Leslie's authority. That might not be the best of ideas. "We'll get your mommy's approval before we ride."

"She'll say no."

"But she must let you do lots of fun things." He wasn't about to fall into the trap of competing with Leslie. "So show me those favorite toys your mother was talking about."

"It's just kid stuff. You wouldn't like it."

"I was a kid once."

Jaci didn't look convinced. She went to the shelf and pulled out a basket of Lego. "I like to build things."

"What kind of things?"

"Towers. As tall as I can. And bridges. They're the hardest."

"I bet."

"How come you went away for so long? Joey's daddy comes home every night and they go to the park and play. Sometimes they take me with them."

"I had an important job to do that was too far away to come home every night, but I'm here now and I'm not going anywhere. How about you show me that park after lunch?"

For a half second he thought she was going to smile, but the curve to her lip turned downward as quickly as it had appeared.

"Lunch is ready."

Pierce looked up. Leslie was standing in the doorway, her arms crossed over her chest, her expression troubled.

Leslie crossed the room and put a hand on Jaci's shoulder. "Go wash up, sweetie. Your dad and I will meet you in the kitchen in a few minutes."

Jaci marched off. The tension in the room soared. Pierce figured the moment of truth had come, but he stayed silent. Always better to know the enemy's position before you sprang into action.

"I thought this could wait until after lunch," Leslie said, "but I'm not good at these games."

"I'm not too keen on them myself." Especially when he didn't know the rules of engagement. "Don't spare my feelings. I'm a big boy. Hit me with it."

"I'm planning to remarry in the spring. I felt you should know."

"Is the groom anyone I know?"

"Does it matter?"

"Probably not."

He waited for the sting of betrayal. Or rejection. Or whatever a guy was supposed to feel when his wife of six years told him she'd replaced him with someone new. It didn't come.

He'd known it was over for months, would have been even if there wasn't another man in the picture.

They'd tried the last couple of times they were together—at least he'd given it a halfhearted shot. Things had gone fine in bed from his standpoint. Leslie was a beautiful, sexy woman.

The problem was there was just no connection anywhere else. He'd actually been glad when his leave was over.

Except for leaving Jaci. It always hurt like hell to say goodbye to Jaci.

She was three months old when he saw her for the first time. He'd been anxious, afraid he wouldn't bond, nervous that he'd be expected to hold her or even tend her alone.

And then he'd peeked into the crib and she'd kicked her tiny feet, waved her pudgy arms and smiled up at him. His heart had melted like a slab of butter in a hot skillet.

The sting he'd expected a few seconds earlier finally hit. Struck everywhere at once, pain scalding his skin and burning his insides, the way it had on that pitch-black night when he and his team members had crawled through the mud into a bed of huge fire ants.

Leslie was welcome to a new life with anyone she chose, but he would not just turn over his parental rights like Jaci was a prize in a competition. Might as well get that straight right now.

"I'm good with you remarrying, but I left the navy SEALs to come home and be a father to Jaci. I am going to be in her life, and not just as a bystander who gets to show up a couple times a year at your convenience."

"I didn't expect that you would, though you missed the first five years by choice."

"That's not fair. I served my country. I was with you and Jaci every opportunity I had."

"That's a moot point now, but you should know that Dan and I will be moving to Cuba next week."

"Cuba? You're moving to Cuba?"

"Temporarily. Dan works for a wealthy developer and is researching possible business opportunities now that the two countries have reopened ties."

The impact of her words hit with dizzying force. His muscles tensed.

"You can't take Jaci to Cuba without my permission. I'm her father. I have rights."

"I haven't threatened your rights, at least not yet."

"If you try to leave the country with her, you better be ready for the fight of your life."

"Keep your voice down. You'll upset Jaci." Leslie closed the bedroom door. "If all goes as planned, Dan will finish the assignment and we'll be back in the States within six months."

"So you worked out all the details before you even ran this by me?"

"It's come up suddenly. I haven't even mentioned this to Jaci yet."

Pierce stabbed his hands deep into the front pockets of his jeans. He was angry, frustrated. And now he was confused. "When do you plan to spring it on her, when you're boarding the plane?"

Leslie sighed and shook her head. "If you'd just let me explain."

"Go right ahead."

"Of course, I had planned to take her with me. I had no other choice, since you were never around."

"I'm here now."

"Yes, and Dan and I have talked about that at length. If you're willing to care for Jaci until I'm back in the States, we can work out a temporary custody arrangement that puts you in charge of Jaci's care."

He couldn't have heard that right. "You'll give me custody of Jaci?"

"Shared custody, actually. But she can live with you, that is, if you think you can be a reliable full-time parent. It is time she gets to know her father."

Jaci would live with him. Full-time for the next six months. He'd be responsible for her. When she was sick. When she cried. When she had nightmares. When she was hungry.

She was only five. She probably still needed help with even the little things like her bath and getting dressed. And with brushing her hair. He'd never brushed anyone's hair in his life. He wouldn't know how to start.

"If you don't want her—"

"No," he interrupted quickly. "It's not that." His head was spinning. "Jaci barely knows me. She clearly doesn't like or trust me. How will it affect her if she thinks I took her away from you?"

"She won't think that. We'll tell her of the decision together, convince her this will be a great adventure for the two of you to share. I need this, Pierce. Dan wants me with him. I want to be with him."

Her voice had taken on a desperate edge. Obviously, new man Dan wielded a powerful influence over her.

"I've raised Jaci practically by myself, Pierce. It's your turn to take some of the responsibility for our child."

He couldn't argue with that and deep inside he didn't want to. He'd come home to bond with his daughter, to be a real father like his father had been before death had claimed him years before his time.

Jaci would live with him. He would be solely responsible for her care, her health, her happiness. It was the scariest challenge he'd ever faced in his life, and that was saying a lot.

He might no longer technically be a SEAL, but he was in his heart. Now it was time to put that same energy and commitment into being a full-time father.

Failure was not an option.

Bring it on.

Chapter Three

"You have got to be kidding. Your wife, who barely let you speak to your daughter on Skype, much less on the phone for the past six months, is suddenly going to toss her to you like a deflated football?"

"Poor analogy, but that's about the size of it," Pierce said as his brother Riley questioned the current scenario. He changed his phone to his left hand, picked up his half-finished beer with his right and took a swig.

"But I can't say much against Leslie. I know she loves Jaci and I think she really wants our daughter not to be traumatized by the divorce."

"I hope that works out for all of you. When did this custody offer come down?" Riley asked.

"Two days ago when I arrived in Chicago."

"You've been back in the good old USA two days and you're just now getting in touch with me?"

"No. I texted you two days ago and again yesterday. Do you ever check your messages?"

"Every now and then."

"Where are you anyway?" Pierce asked. "Tucker said last he heard you were in Colorado."

"That was four or five months ago. I'm in Montana now. Too long in one place and people start thinking you're permanent."

"By 'people' you mean women?"

"And the occasional employee. Actually, I've been on a cattle drive up into the mountains. Wide-open spaces and the biggest, bluest sky you can imagine."

"Tucker said you'd be somewhere hanging out with cows and horses."

"It's in my blood. And his, I might add. How is our younger brother anyway?"

"Still chasing the next rodeo, but having a pretty good year according to him."

"If he admitted that, he's probably headed to a world championship. But back to the issue at hand. What's Jaci's reaction to being deserted by her mother?"

"She seems okay, though Leslie says Jaci is being excessively clingy since we told her about the arrangement. She sees this as more my fault than her mother's. None of this would be happening if I hadn't come home."

"I hope Leslie isn't feeding into that."

"Not to my knowledge. Leslie keeps assuring her that this is only temporary and that I am going to take her on a grand adventure."

"So what's the adventure?"

"I wish the hell I knew."

"Better come up with something fast. I can't quite picture you playing with her Barbie dolls and going shopping for frilly dresses."

"Neither can I."

"Here's a thought. Forget the little-girl stuff. Get her some jeans and cowboy boots. Take her to a dude ranch."

"She does like cowboys."

"I like the kid better already. You could probably use some new boots and a winter Stetson yourself. Pick up a couple of Western shirts and you'll be good to go. You've always had the swagger."

"And the looks in the family."

"You're delusional. Wait a minute. I'm getting a brain jolt here. Forget the dude ranch. I know exactly where you and Jaci should go on your adventure."

"Hit me with it."

"Texas. Go spend some time with the Kavanaughs. God knows Esther and Charlie were lifesavers when we lost our parents. Not that Jaci has literally lost her mother the way we did, but it must feel almost that way to a five-year-old."

"You know, that's not a half-bad idea. I'd love to see Esther and Charlie. Haven't heard from either of them in almost a year, maybe longer."

"Me, either, but Tucker spent a few days with them last summer when the circuit took him to San Antonio. Said they were still holding the Double K Ranch together and doing fine. Claimed it was just like old times. Except for getting a little older, they hadn't changed a bit."

Pierce considered the option. Spending a few days with Esther and Charlie might be the best place to start his six months of bonding with Jaci. He'd truly love to see them and there was no one's advice on child care he'd trust more than Esther's. She was love itself.

And Charlie. Well, there was no one else like Charlie, either. Contrary as a mule, said what he was thinking and thought everyone should carry their share of the load.

But when your world had come to an end, as Tucker, Riley and Pierce's had when their parents had died instantly in a car crash, Charlie and Esther were the ones who'd stepped in. They'd taken them into their home so they wouldn't be separated, helped them through the grief and given them the courage to go on.

"Don't go getting the big head, but I think you just landed on a capital idea," Pierce said.

"Glad I could help and it's about damn time you get back to your Texas roots, bro."

"You could be right about that, too."

"Keep me posted and good luck with full-time fatherhood."

"Thanks. I'll need it."

Boy, was he going to need it. But at least he had a plan and Texas on his mind.

GRACE TOOK HER right hand from the wheel and massaged her aching neck. It was her third day on the run, keeping to back roads, avoiding towns, stopping only at service stations where she could fill the fuel tank, use the facilities and grab a bite to eat.

She was lonely, frightened, discouraged, sometimes downright angry that life wouldn't give her a break. She'd done the right thing. Persevered on the side of justice. Cooperated with the authorities.

Didn't she deserve a chance at happiness or at least not to live in constant fear that her ex-husband would find a way to exact revenge?

A weariness settled in her bones and her eyelids grew heavy. It was too early to stop for the night, still a good hour left before sundown.

She lowered the window so that the cool air could slap her in the face and hopefully ward off the fatigue. The air had an unfamiliar fragrance. Perhaps hay, she thought, as she spotted rolls of it in the fenced pasture to her left. Cows grazed in one section, several horses roamed another.

A strand of towering pines was to the right of the car, interspersed with oaks, junipers, sycamores and a few trees she didn't recognize. Scattered leaves clung to the nearly bare branches. Blackbirds gathered on telephone wires. A dog barked in the distance.

She'd never intended to drive south when she'd fled Tennessee. She'd started driving northwest, but winter storms had altered her travel plans. Desperate to put distance between herself and the man who'd snapped her picture in the library, she'd loaded her car and escaped in the middle of the night. Texas had never been in her plans, but here she was, deep in the heart of the Lone Star State, traversing countryside that seemed miles from civilization. But that was only an illusion.

She'd seen the sign and bypassed the small, rural town of Winding Creek less than ten minutes ago. San Antonio was somewhere to the southeast of her. Mexico was due south.

She planned to meander west, get her head on straight and settle her nerves before she made any permanent decision.

Her foot eased on the accelerator and she faded into her thoughts and into a time back before she'd known fear. A time when she'd had friends and her grandparents were still alive. A time when she'd had dreams. A time when she'd slept without nightmares.

Her car began to shake, the jolts yanking her back to attention. Her right tires had left the shoulder. Her grip on the wheel tightened as she fought to get the car back on the road. Once steadied, she realized how close she'd come to veering off the side of a narrow bridge.

She could have killed herself. Crazy when she was pushing so hard because she wanted to stay alive.

She had to stop, take a walk, or maybe a brief nap. Spotting a dirt road up ahead, she slowed to see if it was a driveway or some type of ranch road. It looked more like a road to nowhere.

Only one way to find out. She turned right. The

road was half-washed-out with deep holes and ruts so numerous they were impossible to avoid completely. The land on both sides of the road was fenced and heavily wooded.

After about five minutes, she reached a point where she didn't dare go farther for fear of getting stuck. She opened the door and stepped out. She felt totally isolated, as if she'd driven off the end of civilization.

The quietness was broken only by squawking crows and the inharmonious cadence of what must be hundreds of katydids and tree frogs. A huge blue lizard rested lazily atop a weathered fence post.

Perhaps a walk would do more to get her blood pumping than a nap. Grabbing her bright yellow cardigan, she tossed it over her shoulder.

The weather forecast was for rain and a cold front moving in tonight, but apparently the words *cold front* had a different meaning here than they did in Tennessee. It was supposed to dip into the low forties tonight.

Locking the nondescript compact car she'd traded down for from a used car dealer in Nashville, she made her way down the bumpy road, careful to avoid tripping.

The scenery changed gradually, the woods thinning and then giving way to wide-open pastures. Clusters of cattle dotted the pastoral landscape, most grazing. At one point there were several near the fence line, much larger than they'd seemed from a distance.

Grace loved horseback riding, but had never been on a real ranch before. She didn't favor the idea of being up close and personal with a cow, especially one of those Texas longhorns she'd spotted over the past two days.

The path, or what was left of it, veered right and began to climb. Grace topped a low hill and then stopped to breathe in a few gulps of the clean-smelling air. She could hear the rush of water in the distance, perhaps the river that flowed beneath the bridge she'd almost crashed into.

She used her hand to shield her eyes from the glare of the late-afternoon sun as she scanned for sight of the river. She didn't see it, but surprisingly she spotted a white clapboard house right there in the middle of nowhere.

It sprawled out in all directions, its dark green shutters and front door making it appear almost like an extension of the land. The place looked so homey, so welcoming, Grace felt a twinge in her heart.

She imagined a family inside, the mother at the range preparing dinner or perhaps helping the kids with homework around a wide kitchen table. The man, tired from a day in the fields, watching the evening news. The setting cozy. Loving.

A life Grace would never have.

She turned to leave. A wailing noise stopped her. An animal? The screech of a bird? Surely cows didn't make that sound.

She heard it again. What if it wasn't an animal?

What if someone needed help? There was no way Grace could leave without checking.

Her concern for herself taking a backseat, Grace carefully maneuvered herself through the barbwire and into the pasture, praying she wouldn't confront a cow or, worse, a bull. Adrenaline pulsed through her veins as she raced toward the sound.

As she got closer, the sound became more distinct. Definitely human. A child or a woman. And it was coming from the vicinity of the house.

ESTHER BIT BACK tears and whispered a prayer for help. She tried to stand again, pushing herself up from the hard dry earth. Pain shot through her leg, even worse than before. She fell back to a sitting position.

The right ankle was beet red and already swelling.

It was her own fault. Trying to save herself a trip, she'd tried to fetch too much firewood at once. She would have made it, though, if she hadn't stepped in a hole some darn critter had dug right there by the woodpile.

Her ankle had twisted, the heavy load had thrown her off balance and she'd toppled like a tower of kids' blocks.

Her fault, but how was she to know that hauling firewood was so tricky? Charlie had done all the hauling for their entire married life.

Salty tears began to roll down her cheeks—not all from the pain in her ankle. She missed Charlie. The house was too quiet without him, her life too lonely.

Feeling sorry for herself wasn't going to solve anything. Staying outside with the forecast of rain and a cold front coming in was unthinkable. Not to mention that the gnats and mosquitoes would eat her alive.

She'd just have to suck up the pain and drag herself to the back door and into the house. She wiped the tears from her eyes with the sleeve of her shirt.

But just in case her hired wrangler, Buck Stalling, hadn't already left for the day, she'd yell one last time.

"Help! Helllp!"

"I'm coming. Hold on. I'm coming."

Esther almost jumped out of her skin. That was a woman's voice, unfamiliar. She wasn't expecting company and she hadn't heard a car drive up.

Maybe she was just imagining things. A sad state of affairs that would be.

"Where are you?"

Definitely a voice. "I'm around back," she called.

A young woman she'd never seen before appeared from around the side of the house. When she spotted Esther, she hurried over.

"Are you hurt? What happened?"

The fierce panic she'd been feeling melted away like a snowball in a sweaty hand.

"I was fetching a heavy load of firewood. Couldn't see where I was walking and stepped in a hole."

The stranger kneeled beside Esther and lightly touched the spot that radiated pain. "Looks like you sprained your ankle. Is that where it hurts?"

"It is. Smarts right bad," Esther said.

"I'm sure. How long have you been out here?"

"Seems like hours but probably only twenty minutes or so."

"We need to get you inside and get some ice on the ankle to slow down the swelling."

"I'm for that." Esther studied the woman, still puzzled by her just showing up out of nowhere. "I'm mighty glad to see you, but who are you and where did you come from? I didn't hear a car drive up."

"I was on the dirt road that borders your ranch and I heard your calls for help."

"That old logging road. Nobody uses that anymore except teenagers riding those racket-making ATVs or else looking for a place to make out. What were you doing there?"

"I was just passing through the area and got too sleepy to keep going. I got out of the car before the road got too bad and took a walk to get the kinks out of my neck and shoulders."

"And you heard me from the logging road? That's 'bout nigh a miracle."

"I barely heard you. At first I thought it was an animal in distress. Luckily, I decided to check it out."

"Luckier for me, and that's a fact. I s'pect those prayers I was saying did some good."

"Couldn't have hurt."

"What's your name?" Esther asked.

"Grace…" She bit her bottom lip as if she'd just uttered a curse word she wished she could take back. She hesitated. "Grace Addison."

"That fits," Esther said. "I needed me some grace today and you showed up."

"Timing is everything," Grace agreed.

"I'm Esther. Esther Kavanaugh. Been living here on the Double K Ranch for years and don't remember ever just tripping, falling and not being able to get up."

"It can happen to anyone. Let's get you inside, and then we can chat."

"I don't know how a little thing like you is gonna help me inside. I'm twice your size."

"That's a major exaggeration, but an additional person for support might make it less painful for you. Were you calling for your husband? If he's around, perhaps I can find him."

Esther shook her head. "Charlie's dead. If he was alive, I wouldn't have been out here in the first place. He took care of me and I took care of him. That's how it always was."

"I'm sorry."

Esther struggled to steady the grief that had snuck into her voice. "Not your fault. It's somebody's, just not yours."

"Who were you calling for?" Grace asked.

"My hired help, but if he were still at the ranch, he'd have heard me yelling before now."

"Then looks like you'll have to trust me to get you inside. Believe me, I'm stronger than I look. But if it hurts too much even with my help, I'll call 9-1-1."

"Don't want no part of that. All those medical people know to do with people my age is take us to the hospital. Then they want to charge us for nothing."

"Then lean against me and try to keep your weight off the right foot while I help you up." Grace took Esther's arm and helped her to a standing position. "Nice and easy. Let me know if the pain seems unbearable."

Esther did as she was told. Thankfully, her Good Samaritan had told the truth. She was a lot stronger than she looked. Esther hobbled along with Grace's help.

"We need to take the steps slowly," Grace said as they reached the back door to the house. "Hold on to the railing with your free hand to help you stay balanced."

Following Grace's advice, Esther took the three back steps with a lot less pain than she'd feared. Nothing seemed quite as scary since Grace had appeared. Of course, once they were inside, Grace would be on her way and Esther would be alone again.

Always alone without Charlie. Someday someone would pay for that. Esther wouldn't rest until justice was done.

But right now she was just grateful for Grace.

Chapter Four

By all rights, Grace should be a nervous wreck at this point. She'd made a major faux pas in the back-yard. She hadn't given anyone her real last name in the six years she'd been on the run. Thankfully, she'd caught herself in time to use the last name that was on her latest fake ID.

It was the unexpected nature of the encounter with Esther. Normally, she planned her life carefully, taking no chances with strangers.

In spite of that, Grace felt at ease. Esther was so sweet and unassuming, her house so cozy, it was impossible not to feel at home with her.

Esther was resting at least semicomfortably now, reclined on the sofa in the loose-fitting cotton robe Grace had helped her change into. Her leg was propped on multiple pillows, her ankle iced and a clean compression wrap from Esther's first aid kit in place.

"Are you a nurse?" Esther asked.

"No, but I've had experience with sprained ankles,

usually my own. But if this is not a lot better by morning, you should see a doctor and have it x-rayed."

"It can't help but be better the way you're pampering me."

"I'm just doing what anyone would do." Grace tucked an available afghan around Esther's legs. "Do you have some pain relievers in the house?"

"I have some ibuprofen I use when the arthritis starts acting up."

"It wouldn't hurt to take that. Where would I find it?"

"In the kitchen cabinet next to the sink and above the counter."

"I'll get it," Grace offered. "Would you like anything else, perhaps a cup of tea?"

"Nothing yet, but you help yourself to anything you see in there that you want. There's homemade chocolate chip cookies in the cookie jar and sweet tea in the refrigerator."

"Thanks, but I had a late lunch." Chips and a soft drink, if you could call that lunch.

Alone in the kitchen, Grace took a few seconds to absorb her surroundings. The kitchen, like the rest of the house, had a cozy, lived-in feel. A red teakettle sat on the back burner of a freestanding gas range. An electric coffeepot was on the counter next to a chicken-shaped sugar bowl and a basket of unshelled pecans.

A breakfast nook with a view of a pumpkin patch

held a round oak table and four captain's chairs topped with blue-and-white-checked cushions.

A sky blue fruit bowl filled with apples, oranges and bananas rested in the middle of the table. The fruit was too tempting to resist. Since Esther had offered, Grace washed her hands at the kitchen sink and helped herself to a banana.

Everything was much as Grace had imagined it when she'd first seen the house from the logging road except that there were no children, no husband, no food simmering on the range. Yet Grace was almost certain the house had once known laughter and great love.

And now she was fantasizing, relying on her own needs to dictate the unknown.

She took a bite of the banana and checked the refrigerator to see if there was something a lousy cook like herself could prepare for Esther's supper. Bacon, eggs and sandwich fixings were plentiful, but that was about it.

The freezer told a different tale. One shelf was filled with serving-size packages of food, all neatly labeled. Soups, meatloaf, chicken and dumplings, casseroles.

Another shelf held sealed plastic bags filled with frozen vegetables. Butter beans, several kinds of peas, corn, carrots and okra, to name a few. Definitely no shortage of food choices.

Satisfied Esther wouldn't starve, Grace quickly went about the business at hand. She finished her banana and retrieved the bottle of pills. She shook out two into her hand and filled a glass with ice water before hurrying back to the large family room.

Esther raised up on her elbows, took the meds and almost finished the glass of water.

"You've done enough waiting on me for now," Esther said. "I'd appreciate if you could stay awhile, but you'd best go get your car before it gets dark."

"Good idea," Grace agreed. "And then I'll come back and warm up something for your dinner."

"For my supper," Esther said. "That's what Charlie always called it. He liked his big meal at lunch and something light at night."

"Then I'll fix your supper," Grace said. "Are you sure you'll be all right while I'm gone?"

"I'm not getting off this sofa. But you can't go traipsing across that pasture and climbing through barbwire again," Esther announced. "You could get hurt."

"I'll be careful." Though she wasn't looking forward to the possibility of meeting a bull head-on.

"Fiddle-faddle. Hand me the phone. I'll call Buck. Much as I have to pay that boy to do a few chores, won't hurt him to do me a favor."

Which bought up a more important subject. Grace handed her the phone. "Speaking of favors, is there someone you can call to stay with you tonight?"

"Don't need 'em. I can hobble the few steps to the bathroom when the urge hits and to the kitchen to get fresh ice when I need it. Rest of the time, I may just sleep right here on the sofa."

"You are a very independent woman, Esther Kavanaugh."

"When you're alone, you have to be."

Grace knew that all too well. Still, she didn't feel good about leaving Esther alone tonight.

Esther made the call to Buck and then turned back to Grace. "His mom says he's in the shower, but she'll send him over as soon as he's dressed."

"Perhaps either Buck or his mother could stay with you tonight," Grace suggested.

"Buck's fine with the livestock. I don't want him trying to help me, though. He's all legs and awkward as all get-out."

"What about his mother?"

"Libby would just keep me awake blabbering all night. She's the biggest gossip in Winding Creek, and that's saying a lot."

"Perhaps there's someone else, then."

"No one I'd like putting up with. You said you were just traveling through. Where are you heading?"

Time for the lies to commence. Fortunately, Grace had worked out most of the details of her new identity while driving. Of course, she'd already blown the fake name.

Being prepared didn't make the lying any easier, especially to someone as open and trusting as Esther.

"I lost my job in Houston," Grace said, "so I'm

going to visit a friend in Albuquerque. She thinks she can get me a job there."

"You're kind of off track for Albuquerque, aren't you?"

"Yes, but since I'm in no hurry, I thought I'd see more of Texas, take back roads, stop at towns I'd never been to."

"Like Winding Creek?"

"Winding Creek wasn't on my original itinerary," Grace admitted, "but I like this part of Texas."

"Most folks do love the Hill Country. So what's your hurry? Stick around a day or two. Drive into Winding Creek. It's a genuine Western town. Still has places on Main Street to hitch your horse—not that I recommend taking a horse into town."

"Perhaps I'll come back one day and check it out."

"No time like the present. I've got plenty of room in this rambling old house and I'd love the company."

"Aren't you afraid I'll blab too much?" Grace teased.

"Wouldn't mind if you did. At least it wouldn't be the same old stories and gossip I've been listening to for years."

"I'm a stranger," Grace said. "You know nothing about me. You really shouldn't invite strangers into your home."

"I know plenty about you. You climbed through a barbwire fence and ran to the aid of someone yelling their lungs out when you had no idea what you might be getting into."

"Anyone would have done that."

"No. Not these days. Well, they do in Winding Creek, but not everywhere. Don't matter, you seem like a good person to me and I'm an excellent judge of character. Even Charlie used to admit that I can spot a liar the second they open their mouth. I can spot an honest person even quicker."

Which didn't bode well for Grace, since almost every word out of her mouth from here on out would be based on a lie. But she did hate the idea of leaving Esther alone tonight.

What harm could one night do? It wasn't as if she was being followed. She'd been far too careful for that. There was no earthly reason for anyone to look for her here.

"I have four extra bedrooms," Esther encouraged. "One ought to be to your liking. None of them are fancy, but the beds are comfortable—even have clean sheets on them. Beats driving an hour or more and then being stuck in some stuffy old motel room down the highway."

"You are putting up a good argument."

"Then it's settled. You'll spend the night here. We'll get to know each other better. I have a feeling we're going to be great friends."

Grace was certain the prediction they'd become friends would never come to fruition. Keeping her past and true identity locked away like bones in a crumbling crypt never allowed her to get too close to anyone.

"Okay," Grace agreed. "One night, if you really want me to stay. But you have to promise to let me take care of you. I don't want you trying to play hostess on that ankle."

"I'm just going to lie right here except when I have to go to the bathroom." Esther smiled and the lines in her face softened as she readjusted her leg on the pillow.

Grace had made the right decision—at least for Esther.

As long as Esther never discovered that the woman she knew as Grace Addison only existed as a character in a horror tale.

GRACE WOKE FROM a sound sleep to a blinding flash of lightning that seemed only inches from her window. An earsplitting crash of thunder followed. She shivered and pulled the quilt up to her chin, not that she expected to go back to sleep with a thunderstorm raging.

She reached for her phone to check the time. Ten past three. Lightning struck again and the accompanying thunder was so loud it rattled the windows.

Esther was at the other end of the long hall. The storm had surely woken her, too. Better go check on her, since that was why Grace was there. If nothing else, she could get her a fresh ice pack.

She flicked on the lamp, shoved her feet into her slippers and pulled on her pink fleece robe, glad she'd remembered to grab it when she'd packed so hurriedly.

Grace was already in the hallway when she remembered the horrid wig she'd been wearing when she'd arrived.

If she'd had any idea she'd be staying in someone else's home even for a night, she would have made another choice. Perhaps a freaky dye job and a short, spiky haircut. She could have gone goth. She still might when she left the Double K Ranch.

Rain began to pelt the windowpanes. Grace grabbed the wig from the top of the antique dresser and pulled it low on her head. She adjusted and readjusted until she was certain none of her own brown locks escaped the wig.

Reminding herself she was Grace Addison, she tiptoed to Esther's bedroom. Her door was ajar. Esther's whistling snores overrode the sounds of the torrential rain. Perhaps that was why the storm hadn't awoken her.

The temperature in the house was several degrees cooler than it had been when Grace had gone to bed and she could feel a chilly draft in the hallway. She'd made certain the front and back doors were closed and locked, but the draft had to be coming in somewhere.

She followed the chill to the family room and turned on the overhead light. It took only a few seconds to discover the problem. A window behind the sofa was open a crack and the wind and rain were blowing in.

Grace closed and locked the window, then went to the bathroom to get a towel to wipe up the water.

Another bolt of lightning hit, this one cutting a path straight downward as if the house itself were the target. Thunder roared. The light blinked twice and then went out.

A suffocating sensation sucked the air from Grace's lungs as pitch-blackness closed in around her.

It had been storming like this the night this had all started. Almost six years ago. A night of terror that refused to let her go. The memories crawled from beneath the darkest recesses of her mind and she was back there again.

Lying alone in the king-size bed, silk sheets skimming her naked body. Surrounded by opulence. Drowning in suspicions she could no longer deny.

Her dreams died that night and the never-ending nightmare began.

Grace made her way back to the bedroom in the dark and climbed beneath the covers. The storm still raged on outside, but the real upheaval was inside her soul.

"LAND O' GOSHEN, you're just as busy as a buzz saw in a pine knot, Grace. I swear you haven't stopped working since you woke up."

"I haven't actually accomplished that much."

"Cooked my breakfast, cleaned up the kitchen, ran the vacuum cleaner, washed and dried sheets and towels, straightened my little nest here on the sofa and waited on me like I was the Queen of England. I'd say that's a powerful lot."

"I like to stay busy, and I have to earn my keep. After all, you did provide me a port in the storm last night."

"It was you who did me the favor. I'm not afraid to admit that ankle had me worried. I was afraid something was broken. I sure didn't need that."

"I'm glad it's better this morning, but you shouldn't overdo it. It would be helpful if you had a walker or at least a cane you could use for support."

"You know, I think Charlie's cane might still be in the closet of one of those spare bedrooms. He bought it after he had his right knee replaced a couple of years back."

"I'll take a look before I leave and see if I can find it. Right now, it's time for you to have a fresh ice pack on the ankle again. Are you ready?"

"How long do we have to keep doing that?"

"At least another twenty-four hours. You want to avoid as much swelling as possible."

"Good thing I like purple," Esther said. "Looks like I might get about ten shades of it when those bruises burst into full bloom."

"That you may."

Grace went for the ice pack and adjusted it on Esther's ankle.

"I hope you don't think I'm taking advantage of you," Esther said.

"I'd never think that. I'm going to check and see

if I can find that cane, and then I need to get back on the road. Is there anything else I can do for you before I go?"

"Well, there is one favor that would mean a lot to me. Not exactly a favor, 'cause I'll pay you what I can."

"What is it?"

Esther sucked in her bottom lip and put her palms to her cheeks as if she were afraid to say what was on her mind.

"Just ask me," Grace encouraged. "I don't promise I can say yes, but I won't be upset with you for asking."

"I was thinking maybe I could get you to stay with me a week or so—perhaps through Christmas. This whole holiday thing is about to get me down. Every time I think about it, I start crying."

Esther's eyes grew moist and a lone tear escaped and rolled down her right cheek.

Grace's heart warmed, melting her good sense with it. "Is this your first Christmas without Charlie?"

Esther nodded "He's been dead three months. I figured I could ignore the holiday, but Charlie loved Christmas. He'd hate to see me doing without a tree and decorations. I can't really ignore Christmas anyway. People send cards, and every time I turn on the TV or the radio, they're talking about the holidays.

"Can't even go to the grocery market in Winding Creek without seeing the garlands and stars hanging from the streetlights. I always loved Christmas, but it won't be the same without Charlie."

"Don't you have any family you could stay with?" Grace asked.

"No, Charlie and I never had kids. We wanted 'em. It just never worked out for us to have them. Closest thing to family we had were the Lawrence boys. They lived with us for ten months a few years back. My, did we love those boys. But they're all grown up now, scattered around the world and busy with their own lives. Sure would be nice if you could stay through Christmas."

Grace hated to turn down such a simple request when she had nowhere to go. But staying there meant continuously lying to a woman who trusted her. And there was always a chance it could put Esther in danger.

But if Grace didn't leave the ranch, how could anyone know she was there? On the surface it seemed a great place to go unnoticed.

"If you can't do it, I understand," Esther said. "It was just a thought."

"Not a bad thought," Grace admitted.

Not that she was ever in the best of moods at Christmas herself. She usually spent the holiday in pajamas, watching old Christmas movies and crying.

"I can't promise I can stay through Christmas," Grace said. She could never make promises. "But I'll stay another day. We'll see where it goes from there."

"It's gonna go good," Esther said. "It's gonna go real good. I can feel it in my bones."

"But no talk of money," Grace stressed. "I consider us friends now and I want to help."

"You don't know what this means to me."

"Just don't count on my being here for Christmas. Is there anything else I can do for you before I go search for the cane?"

"I hate to keep making you work," Esther said, "but it would sure be nice if you'd gather the eggs from the henhouse."

Gather eggs. Grace had done that many times as a kid—at Easter with no chickens directly involved. That was obviously not what Esther meant.

"I have some rubber boots you can wear so you don't get your shoes all muddy after last night's storm."

"I'll be glad to help, but I'll need a bit more instruction."

"Are you telling me you've never gathered fresh hen eggs?" Esther's shock showed.

"Never."

"Then you're in for a real treat." Esther smiled conspiratorially and motioned to Grace to come sit down on the sofa by her. "You're not afraid of chickens, are you?"

"Should I be?"

"Not if you want eggs to eat. I have a large basket sitting on the work shelf in the mudroom. Just take it with you to the chicken coop. You can't miss the henhouse. Step inside it and you'll see two rows of straw-filled nests. Just reach in the nests and take the eggs."

It sounded simple enough. "The chickens don't mind?"

"They're used to it. If there's a chicken sitting in the nest, don't disturb her. She'll cackle and move on when she's done. Then you can go back to that nest."

"So I just reach in the nests and collect the eggs?"

"That's it. I refilled their water containers yesterday, so you don't have to worry with that. They'll probably be drinking out of the mud puddles today anyway."

"Is that safe?"

"It is if you're a chicken."

"What about feed?"

"There will still be some mush in the automatic feeder. But stop at the woodshed on your way to the chicken yard."

"The woodshed?"

"Yes, it's right behind where I fell last night. Be sure you latch the shed when you leave. Otherwise, the door will blow open and the deer will make short work of the corn and feed stored in there."

"I can handle that."

"You'll see a metal container in the shed—on the shelf above a pail of whole kernel corn. Fill the container with the kernels or you can just drop a few handfuls into your jacket pockets."

"What do I do with the corn?"

"Toss it around the chicken pen and the chickens will come running."

Chickens running at her. Better than cows or bulls, but the image wasn't comforting.

"Is it too late to change my mind about my offer of help?" Grace teased.

"Yes, but don't worry. Gathering the eggs is fun. You'll miss it when you do leave."

Grace seriously doubted that.

"Okay, basket by the back door. Corn in the woodshed. Now, where are these chickens?"

"Take the path behind the woodshed and you'll run right into the chicken pen. Can't miss it. You'll hear the clucking before you get there."

"Is the pen locked?"

Esther laughed. "No need, neither the chickens nor the foxes can work the latch."

"There are foxes out there?"

"Foxes, coyotes, hawks, an occasional bobcat. They love chicken. But they're not fond of humans, so you won't see any of them. Oh, and there's a big red barn off to the left of the pen. If you see someone out there, don't worry. It'll be Buck. He's supposed to haul some hay out to the north pasture today."

A few minutes later, Grace was heading for the chicken pens, woven basket in hand, pockets full of corn. She was feeling more confident by the minute.

How difficult could gathering eggs be?

When she reached the coop, she unlatched and opened the wire gate. Several hens came running at her. She stood her ground. But she'd wait to scatter the corn until she'd gathered the eggs. Then she could toss the kernels and make a fast getaway before all of the hens were advancing on her.

The basket firmly in hand, Grace stepped inside the red-roofed coop. Sure enough there were two rows of nests, lined with hay.

Several hens were scratching around on the ground beneath the nests. One beautiful red hen sat on a nest like a queen on her throne.

"I'm not messing with you, sister," Grace said calmly. "You just go about your business."

The hen ignored her. Grace moved down the line and began to gather eggs, careful not to break them. For some reason she'd expected them all to be the same color even though the chickens weren't. The eggs ranged from snowy white to a speckled brown.

By the time her basket was full, she was feeling pretty proud of herself. Gathering eggs. Nothing to it.

The hen on the nest cackled loudly. Then she left the nest and marched back into the yard. One more egg for the basket that was almost full.

Grace walked to the gate, the basket full of eggs hanging over her arm. She undid the latch and reached into her pocket for the corn. Maybe she wouldn't run. The chickens seemed harmless enough.

She grabbed a handful of kernels and tossed them into the dirt. Chickens came running from every corner of their fenced pen. They quickly gobbled up the corn but didn't bother her.

She took a few steps away from the gate and was about to scatter the rest when she noticed a giant rooster heading right for her.

His neck was bobbing. His spurs were twice as big as the hens' and looked like they should be classified as deadly weapons. The bright red comb on his head and the loose skin at his neck seemed like he was waving a warning flag.

He stopped between her and the gate and made a *tuck, tuck, tuck, tuck* sound. Not good. Probably a call for attack. He jumped toward her.

Grace started to run. The rooster stayed right behind her. The eggs she'd so carefully gathered began to tumble from her basket.

Throw the corn. Quick. Toss it as far as you can and make a run for the gate.

She slowed to grab a handful of kernels. Her foot slipped and she went sliding, landing on her butt right in the middle of a mud puddle.

Finally, she threw the corn as far as she could. The rooster and all the hens followed the food. By now half of the eggs were on the ground, cracked. She was covered in mud. And the crazy wig had slid down so that it practically covered her eyes.

This couldn't possibly get any worse.

She started to get up and slipped again. Muddy water splattered her face and the lens of her glasses.

And then she heard laughter. Hardy, deep, full-throated laughter. She looked up and into the face of one of the hunkiest, most gorgeous men she'd ever seen.

She'd been wrong. Things had just gotten a lot worse.

Chapter Five

Pierce struggled to squelch his laughter as he hurried over to see if he could help. He wasn't laughing at the fall, though thankfully she didn't appear to be hurt.

It was the image of her sloshing through the mud with a rooster and half the chickens in the pen chasing after her for their corn. It was the eggs tumbling from her basket like jumping beans. And that ugly, lopsided wig.

As he opened the gate, the laughter escaped again.

"It wasn't that funny," she quipped as he approached her.

"Sorry, I shouldn't have laughed, but..."

Damn, he couldn't help himself. He tried to swallow the chuckle that didn't want to let go of him. "Actually, it was pretty funny from my viewpoint," he admitted.

"If you videotaped it for YouTube, I'll kill you."

"No pictures, I swear."

She was a lot younger than he'd thought from a

distance. And the brown hair that had escaped the wig was shiny, nothing like the frizzy black wig.

"Are you hurt?" he asked.

"Just my pride." She wiped the mud from her right hand onto her jeans. Then she changed the basket to her right hand and did the same with her left hand. He thought she might be planning to shake hands with him, but she made no such move.

Couldn't blame her. But the show had been hilarious.

He pulled a clean handkerchief from his back pocket and handed it to her. "This might help."

She took off the glasses and stuck them in her pocket, then used his handkerchief to wipe her face, though mostly it just smeared the mud around like black war paint.

He reached down, pushed her wig back up her forehead.

"What's with the wig? Were you going incognito so the rooster wouldn't recognize you?"

"How is that any of your business?"

"Point made." Probably not a good time to talk about a woman's appearance when she was splattered with mud.

Jaci finally joined them. She stuck her hands on her hips and stared up defiantly at the mud-encrusted woman.

"Why did you steal those chickens' eggs? That's not nice."

"I didn't steal them," the woman protested. "I was just taking them into the house."

"They belong to the chickens. That's stealing."

"You're right and believe me I won't do it again if I can help it." The woman started retrieving the few unbroken eggs from the ground.

"It's not stealing," Pierce assured Jaci. "The chickens lay eggs for us to eat. The eggs we buy at the store come from chickens, too."

Obviously dissatisfied with the explanation, Jaci tugged on the tail of the woman's jacket until she stopped gathering the eggs and looked down at her.

"If you didn't steal the eggs, why were all the chickens chasing you?"

"Good question. Ask the chickens."

"Chickens can't talk, can they, Daddy?"

"Not any language that I can speak."

One by one, Pierce stepped on the broken eggs, grinding them under the toe of his boot until the shells were ground like sand and the liquid disappeared into the wet earth.

"Why are you smashing the eggs?" Jaci asked, already joining him in the task.

"So the chickens don't realize they're good to eat. Then they might eat all the eggs and not leave any for us."

"So you're an expert on chickens as well as women's wigs," the woman quipped.

"I'm a multitalented guy."

"No doubt."

"Truth is I learned about chickens the same way you just did—the hard way. And in this same pen."

He picked up the last two good eggs and placed them in her basket. "I'm Pierce Lawrence and this is my curious daughter, Jaci."

"I'm Grace Addison." Her tone lost some of its sarcastic edge. "Are you a friend of Esther's?"

"Practically family."

"Really? Then you must be one of the famous Lawrence boys Esther mentioned."

"More like the *infamous* Lawrence boys. And *family* might be a slight exaggeration, since I haven't been around in quite a while." They left the pen and Pierce latched it behind them. "Give me a minute to grab our luggage from the truck and we'll walk back to the house with you."

Grace glanced toward the black double-cab pickup truck he'd bought new in Chicago.

"Why are you parked way out here if you came to see Esther?"

"I wanted to test my new truck on a rough ranch road before I tried it on more rugged terrain."

He opened the truck and pulled out a child's backpack.

Jaci reached for it. "I can carry my own toys. I'm strong," she said.

"Good thing. This backpack is really heavy," Pierce said, playing along. He helped Jaci fit it on her back, then pulled two duffels from the backseat and slung one over each arm.

"That's it?" Grace asked.

"Cowboys travel light. Right, Jaci?"

"I'm a cowgirl."

"How could I forget?"

They started back to the house. "Esther didn't mention that she was expecting you," Grace said.

"I haven't talked to Esther or Charlie in months," Pierce admitted. "Actually, I haven't been in this area in years. I thought I'd surprise them."

"I'm so sorry. You must not have heard."

She sounded genuinely upset. "What's the problem?"

"Charlie's dead."

"Oh, no. Not Charlie." The news hit hard, and he struggled to get his mind around it. "When did that happen?"

"Three months ago."

"I hadn't heard. Neither have my brothers. It's hard to believe. I mean, he was in great health the last time I saw him. He wasn't that old." Pierce was rambling, talking as much to himself as to Grace. "How did he die?"

"I don't know."

That seemed a bit strange. "How long have you known Esther?"

"Not long," Grace said. "She sprained her ankle yesterday. I'm staying with her a few days to help out. I'm sure she won't trust me gathering eggs again."

"Don't count on that. Esther will just demand you

do it until you get it right. She'll drive you like a team of horses and make you love her for it."

"Thanks for the warning."

"How's Esther doing, I mean without Charlie? They were so close—still held hands and had every meal together. She was the only one who could talk him down when he got really riled about something."

"What kind of things riled him that much?"

"Mistreating one of his animals. People lying to him or not doing what they'd promised. Politics."

"She seems very lonely without him."

"I'm sure. Who's running the ranch? Esther always had her garden and her chickens, shares with all the neighbors, but the livestock was Charlie's baby."

"She's hired a part-time wrangler, a young neighbor guy named Buck. That's all I know."

For a friend, she didn't seem to know much about what was going on around there. And she'd definitely never been around chickens before.

When they reached the house, Pierce was hesitant to climb the back steps and knock. What could he possibly say to Esther that would let her know how sorry he was? He was terrible at that sort of thing.

He looked around for Jaci. She was kicking through the leaves.

Grace held back. "I'll wait for your daughter. You go ahead. It's your surprise. Door's not locked and hopefully she's on the sofa resting that ankle."

The surprise had gone sour after learning of Charlie's death. Esther might not even want to see him after neither he nor his two brothers had stayed in touch close enough to know about Charlie's death.

At least one of his brothers would have been there for the funeral if they'd known. Pierce was there now. He'd have to work with that.

He opened the back door and stepped inside the mudroom. He took off the new Stetson that Riley had encouraged him to buy and slid it onto the hat shelf next to one of Charlie's summer Stetsons.

The sense of loss hit him square on. This was not going to be easy.

"How did the egg gathering go?"

He stood silently at the sound of Esther's voice. She was obviously in the kitchen and thought it was Grace who'd come in the back door.

"Better for the chickens than the gatherer," he said, stepping into the kitchen.

Esther stared at him and then started to tremble. "Pierce Lawrence, is that really you?"

"The one and only."

He didn't bother with words, just did what came naturally. He opened his arms and she stepped inside them. She dissolved into sobs while Pierce blinked back a tear or two of his own.

"I thought you were out of the country," she finally muttered between sobs and sniffles.

"I was. I'm officially discharged and back in the States for good now."

"I knew you'd come when you could, Pierce. I

know how much you loved Charlie. I know how much he loved you."

Jaci stepped into the kitchen alone, only now she was holding the half-empty basket of eggs. She proudly handed them to Esther.

"This is my daughter, Jaci," Pierce said. "We're spending some time getting reacquainted. A road trip to Texas seemed a good way to do that."

"I'm glad you brought her along." Esther placed a wrinkled hand on Jaci's shoulder. "Glad to meet you, young lady. Your dad is one of my favorite people in all the world, so I know you and I will be good friends."

"And, Jaci, this is Esther Kavanaugh, the woman I've told you so much about."

Jaci stared at Esther quizzically. "Are you my aunt, my cousin or my grandmother?"

"What would you like me to be?"

"Well, I only have one grandmother. Joey has two and my friend Penny has three. I need another grandmother."

"I'd love to be your honorary grandmother—if it's all right with your daddy."

"Fine by me," Pierce said.

"What's 'honorary'?" Jaci questioned.

"It means I'm very lucky to be your grandma Esther."

"Do you still have horses?"

"Ah, you like horses, do you?"

"Yes. Daddy's going to teach me to ride."

"That's exciting."

"Where are your horses?"

"A few are probably in the horse barn. Buck has probably let most of them out into their pasture by now, since the rain has cleared out. They like to get outside and play just like little girls do."

Grace finally made it into the kitchen sans her muddy boots and jacket but still with streaks of mud on her face and lower arms. The grotesque wig had been plopped back in place.

Esther gasped. "What happened to you?"

"I'll let Pierce fill you in while I get a shower. He got a much bigger kick out of the happenings than I did. Now, what are you doing in the kitchen when you're supposed to be resting that ankle?"

"I'll see that she gets back to the sofa before I regale her with your chicken gathering adventure," Pierce promised.

Grace rolled her eyes, but she followed that with a smile.

Damn. Eyeglasses that dwarfed her face, mud for makeup and baggy jeans. Still, she looked cute when she smiled. There was probably a real hottie hidden in there somewhere.

Not that it mattered to him. The last thing he needed right now was another woman in his life. Esther and Jaci were going to be challenge enough.

GRACE REJOINED THEM thirty minutes later smelling like flowers and soap. Pierce still didn't have a handle on exactly who Grace was, only that she was staying with Esther temporarily.

He didn't know much more about Charlie's death. The details Esther furnished had been extremely skimpy. When he'd questioned her for more, she'd just motioned toward Jaci, who had climbed up in Charlie's old recliner and was engrossed in games on her iPad.

Esther obviously thought the subject matter unfit for Jaci's ears. He'd find out more when he got her alone.

On the other hand, the little she'd told him about Grace troubled him. She'd just happened to be walking on an old logging road to nowhere when she'd heard Esther call for help. She'd rescued Esther and now she'd temporarily moved in.

What kind of young woman would do that?

Either one who had a heart of gold or someone who expected to get something out of this. But what was she after?

Cash?

Jewelry? As far as he knew, all Esther had was her wedding band.

A place to hide out from the law?

Or maybe she was in danger. On the run. Running from the law or from danger would explain the bad wig and unattractive glasses that kept sliding down the bridge of her nose.

"I know you all have to be hungry by now," Esther said. "It's after noon."

"I could eat," Pierce said.

Esther chuckled. "You could always eat. I took some chicken and dumplings, creamed corn and turnip greens out of the freezer when Grace left to gather eggs. It can all finish defrosting in the warming sauce pans."

"Now we're talking. No one makes chicken and dumplings like you," Pierce said honestly. "I'd have killed for that in Afghanistan."

"If I'd known you were coming, I'd have made a fresh pot instead of feeding you out of the freezer."

"I may have to stick around until you make good on that offer."

Esther pulled her ankle from the pillow and started to stand.

"Oh, no, you don't," Grace protested. "I'll warm the food. You take it easy. The healing process can't be rushed."

"See, Pierce, I told you she's spoiling me rotten."

"As you descrve," Pierce said. That didn't convince him Grace had no ulterior motive. "I'll help in the kitchen," he volunteered, hoping that would give him a chance to feel out the situation.

Jaci looked up from her game. "I don't want to eat lunch. You promised I could ride a horse."

"And we will ride," Pierce said. "Right after we eat, as long as that's okay with Esther."

"You know you can just make yourself at home, Pierce. I think I have everything you need in the tack room."

"We bought her a helmet on the way here," Pierce said. "Also boots and a hat."

"And some cowgirl clothes," Jaci added. She did a 360-degree turn so they got the full effect of her new jeans and Western shirt.

"Nice," Grace acknowledged.

"Then I know we have everything else you need," Esther said, "even a saddle that should be just Jaci's size."

"And you didn't even know we were coming."

"No, but one of our friends from church bought the saddle for when his young grandson visits from California. Charlie taught the boy to ride. Not sure which of them enjoyed that more."

"Yeah. I wish I knew half what Charlie knew about horses," Pierce said.

"I just wish you could have come while he was still alive. You were always his favorite, you know."

Pierce didn't know or believe that. Charlie had always treated him and his brothers the same.

"Will this be your first time to ride a horse, Jaci?" Esther asked.

"I rode a pony one time, but he was hooked to other horses and we just went in a tiny circle. Boring. Daddy is going to let me ride a horse that's not just for birthday parties."

"That's much more exciting," Grace agreed.

"We're on an adventure 'cause Momma went to Cuba. She wouldn't let me go."

"Really? Cuba?" Esther questioned.

Pierce motioned to her to let that subject drop for now. "Are you going to ride a horse, too?" Jaci asked Esther.

"Not today. I used to love to ride, but old bones don't always like bumping around in a saddle."

Jaci ran over and grabbed Grace's hand. "Then will you go with us? Please."

"Maybe I'll watch," Grace said, clearly not excited about the prospect.

Pierce stayed until Esther had filled him in further on which mounts were the most gentle and dependable, and then he joined Grace in the kitchen. She was bent over, rummaging in a lower cabinet for pots. The baggy jeans couldn't hide the fact that she had a dynamite ass. He looked away before the twinge in his groin became more.

"You can get Esther her ice pack while I start warming the food," Grace suggested.

"I can handle that."

Grace emptied the chicken and dumplings into a stew pot. "Will Jaci eat what's on the menu? Or should I look for some peanut butter and jelly or mac and cheese? I know how picky some kids her age can be."

"Hate to say it, but I don't really know what she eats. I've been in the military and out of the country for most of her life. I do know she won't hesitate to let us know if she doesn't like it. She is very opinionated."

"I realized that in the chicken yard."

"Well, it isn't nice to steal eggs from cute little chickens."

Grace wadded the paper towel she was wiping her hands on and threw it at him.

He put up his hand and caught it. "Gotta be quicker than that to catch a former SEAL off guard."

"Or sneaky. You never know what you might get from me."

And that possibility was what worried him the most about Grace Addison.

JACI WAS A precocious and consummate manipulator.

Grace had found it impossible to deny her pleadings that she go with them to watch her first riding lesson.

Pierce seemed right at home, rubbing horses' noses and talking to them like they understood. Grace would have done the same, but she decided to play this smart. If she acted as if she was afraid of the horses, she'd have a good excuse for not going riding with Pierce.

Not that she wouldn't love to ride, but she could sense he was suspicious about why she was there. The last thing she needed was a lot of probing questions.

Pierce lifted Jaci and let her run her fingers through one of the horse's manes.

"Who takes care of the horses on a ranch?" she asked.

"Sometimes the guy who owns the ranch. Sometimes a wrangler who works for him."

"What's a wrangler?"

"A cowboy who takes care of the cattle and horses."

"You could be a wrangler, Daddy. You have cowboy boots and a cowboy hat."

"That's not a bad idea."

Jaci reached out as Pierce moved to the next stall. "What's this one's name, Daddy?"

"Dreamer. See, her name is over her stall."

"Is it a girl or a boy horse?"

"It's a mare, which means she's a girl."

"I think she likes me."

"I think she does, too. And Dreamer is the horse Esther recommended for you. Would you like me to saddle her up so you can ride her?"

"Mommy wouldn't like it."

"She worries about you getting hurt. But I'm here to make sure you don't. I'll be walking with you and holding on to the lunge line."

"What's a lunge line?"

"Kind of like a leash for me to lead Dreamer by so I can make sure you're safe and having a good time in the saddle."

For a man who'd admittedly spent very little time around his daughter, Pierce was amazingly patient with all her questions. He seemed to genuinely enjoy just having her around.

But Grace couldn't help but wonder about his relationship with Jaci's mother, who was apparently on her own adventure in Cuba. Pierce hadn't mentioned a divorce, but he wasn't wearing a wedding band.

None of her business, Grace reminded herself, and she wasn't about to ask. By necessity, everything and everyone on the Double K Ranch was temporary.

The horse closest to Grace snorted loudly and pawed at the ground as if he were ready to bolt and run. She started to try to calm him, then remembered her strategy just in time. She jumped backward.

"Calm down, Huckleberry."

"I'm okay. He just startled me."

"Nonetheless, that was some fancy footwork. Yours—not Huckleberry's."

"I'm not without talents." And now she was flirting, in self-defense, but still flirting. It surprised her she even remembered how.

"Jaci's decided on Dreamer," Pierce said. "Which horse should I saddle for you?"

"It's Jaci's day. I'll just stay out of the way and watch her great adventure."

"You're not afraid of horses, are you?"

"No. Of course not. I love them. Thinking of trading in my car for one."

His mouth curved into a teasing half smile. A heated zing rushed her senses. She fought it into submission.

"Have you ever ridden?" Pierce asked.

"Do carousel ponies count?"

"Not past your fifth birthday."

"Then I guess the answer is no."

"We can't let that go on. We'll come back tomorrow—for a private lesson."

She ignored the comment, but she had no intention of doing anything private with Pierce Lawrence. The kind of charm he oozed would lead to nothing but trouble.

"Okay, Jaci, it looks like you're the only one up for a riding lesson."

She clapped her hands in delight. Minutes later, Pierce had Dreamer saddled and ready to go. Grace was standing beside Jaci in a small corral just beyond the horse barn.

Pierce motioned Jaci over. "Dreamer's ready."

Instead of going to Pierce, Jaci clasped Grace's hand. With her free hand, Jaci pulled a lock of her hair from beneath her helmet, stretching it across her lips.

"I changed my mind. I don't want an adventure today, either."

"Nothing to be afraid of," Pierce reassured. "We won't move a step until you tell me you're ready. Let's just try sitting in the saddle. I won't let go of you unless you tell me to."

"You promise?"

"I promise."

Jaci approached Pierce and the horse cautiously.

"Relax," Pierce said. "I won't let you get hurt. This is going to be fun."

Jaci put her hands up for him to lift her into the saddle. Pierce lifted her gingerly and true to his word he kept his hands at her waist to steady her.

In seconds, her nervous expression faded into a huge grin.

Pierce placed the reins in her hands.

She held them up for Grace to see. "I'm a real cowgirl now."

"I believe you are."

Jaci sat straight, head high. "You can let go of me now, Daddy."

He let go and took one step backward, the lunge line in his right hand.

"Giddyup," Jaci called.

Pierce let the lunge line out a few feet and began to lead Dreamer around the corral.

Jaci beamed. "Look, Grace. I'm riding a big horse."

"You are. And you're doing a great job."

So was Pierce. He was obviously a natural at fatherhood. A warmth crept deep inside Grace, followed immediately by a sinking sensation that knotted in her chest. This was a life she might have had. A husband. A child. A circle of love.

The life she would never have. Coveting it, comparing it to what she was forced to settle for, only made the hurt run deeper.

She'd promised Esther to stay a few days, but Pierce and Jaci were here. Esther didn't really need her anymore. She'd just pack up in the morning and move on. It would be best for everyone.

And harder than she would have ever guessed.

Chapter Six

Pierce owed Riley big-time for his suggestion to bring Jaci back to Texas. It would take a lot more time together for Jaci to fully bond with him, but riding Dreamer had definitely jump-started the stalled process.

The sad shocker had been discovering that Charlie was dead. The last time Pierce had seen him, he'd seemed as strong and energetic as a man half his age. Pierce had expected him to be around for years to come. Had a lot he'd planned to share with him about his activities as a SEAL.

His sudden death must have torn the heart right out of Esther and left her incredibly lonely. No wonder she'd taken so fast to a total stranger who'd come to her rescue.

Grace Addison. Mystery woman. Cute in spite of her deliberate efforts to make herself look homely. A quick wit. Easy to be around. Good with Jaci.

But unless he was way off base, she was running

from something or someone. Before he left her here with Esther, he'd get to the bottom of that.

Jaci and Grace were already in the truck waiting while he finished getting fresh water for the horses. He slid behind the wheel, closed the door and started the engine.

"Mind if we take a drive around the ranch before we head back?" Pierce asked. "It's been a long time since I've seen this place I once called home."

"If you'd like," Grace said. "But we shouldn't stay away from the house too long in case Esther needs us."

Jaci didn't answer. She was already hooked up to earphones. He wasn't sure if that was just a sign of the times or her way of escaping him.

Either way, it was a habit he hoped to replace soon with activities that required interaction with him and ensured more exercise than being hooked into an electronic machine.

He took off down the worn dirt road that ran along the fence line. After a hundred yards, he cut off that path for the one that drove through acres and acres of fenced pastureland.

"How are you going to keep from getting lost?" Grace asked. "There aren't any road signs or landmarks."

"Oh, there's plenty of landmarks if you know what you're looking for. See that cluster of cedar trees on the crest just past that lone pine. That's the starting

point for the northwest pasture. Go north from there
and you run into my favorite fishing hole.

"Of course, when I lived here I was usually riding
a horse or one of the ATVs. No one drove Charlie's
pickup truck. He did teach me to drive in it, though,
right here on the ranch."

"Is Charlie the one who laid out these roads?"

"He didn't lay them out per se. They're just the
paths he traveled to get where he wanted to be. Do
that enough and it beats down the dirt and kills the
grass."

"Whoa." She pointed out the window. "What was
that strange-looking creature that just crossed in front
of us?"

"A roadrunner. Have you never seen one before?"

"In cartoons—which makes sense. They are funny
looking."

"And faster than a human. Keep watching. We
may come across some wild turkeys or some giant
jackrabbits."

"How big is the Double K Ranch?"

"Just under twelve thousand acres, if I remember
right. Not particularly a large ranch by Texas stan-
dards, but it's big enough to make a living if you
manage it right, especially since it has lots of good
grazing land."

They rode in silence after that and Pierce became
more concerned by the minute. The ranch was not
kept up the way he remembered. Fences were practically falling down in several places. Some pastures

were overgrazed, though so far he hadn't seen as many cattle as he'd expected. A gate was hanging by one hinge, the other broken off.

He'd noticed that the area around the horse barn needed some work, too. Nothing too costly, but it would take work and time to get things the way Charlie kept them when he was alive.

Pierce spotted a black pickup truck up ahead parked near a guy who was repairing a strand of barbwire. "That must be Buck," Pierce said, slowing and pulling up next to the truck. "I'd like to introduce myself. You guys can wait here or get out and stretch."

Jaci remained in her chosen state of electronic oblivion.

Grace opened her door but didn't get out. "Are there cows and bulls around?"

"Hopefully, and steers, too. Otherwise, you don't have much of a ranch."

"Then I'll wait in the truck."

"Does that mean you're not going to help me feed the cattle later?"

"Don't push your luck, cowboy."

He tipped his hat and swaggered away.

Buck removed his work gloves, reached over the fence and shook hands as they exchanged names.

"So you're Pierce Lawrence. I've heard about you from the Kavanaughs. Navy SEAL hero, right?"

"The navy SEAL part is accurate. I wouldn't put any stock in the hero part."

"Charlie said you saved lives."

"Just doing my job."

"I'm glad you're here," Buck said. "Mrs. Kavanaugh's had a tough time since Charlie died. She says this is the only life she's ever known, but truth is she don't know much about running a ranch."

"I suspected that might be the case."

"I try to explain to her about the kinds and amounts of feed and how the horses need exercise and the barn needs a new room, but she just keeps telling me to make do."

"The ranch was never her thing," Pierce said.

"Well, maybe you can convince her. She's running low on hay. No way are we going to stretch what we've got through the winter."

"I'll check on that and see that it's ordered before I leave."

"That will be a start," Buck said, "but the ranch needs some serious work. I do what I can, but the Double K needs a full-time wrangler. Esther claims she doesn't have the cash for that, so I have to get my hours in on Dudley Miles's spread and then spend the rest of daylight here."

"That explains some of the neglect. I'll talk to her about the issues," Pierce said. "It may be she's just not thinking too clearly with all the grief. I'm sure she's still dealing with Charlie's dying so suddenly."

"Not only that but Mother says she's not even fully recovered from her heart attack."

"Esther had a heart attack?"

"Yeah, a bad one. Happened when she found Charlie's body in the barn."

"I hadn't heard about that," Pierce said. "In fact, I just heard about Charlie's death when I got here today. Was it a heart attack that killed him?"

Buck two-fingered the brim of his Western hat and pulled it lower on his forehead. "I hate to be the one to tell you this, but Charlie committed suicide. Shot himself in the head with his own pistol. Blood was splattered all over the barn."

The images swirled in Pierce's head. For a second he was back on that craggy mountainside in Afghanistan, incoming fire taking out his friends one by one.

But Charlie had been hit by his own bullet. What would have ever possessed him to do such a thing? He loved this ranch. He loved Esther more than life.

"Mother was in the hospital with Mrs. Kavanaugh when they told her Charlie's death was ruled a suicide," Buck said.

"She must have been crushed."

"Worse. She went berserk. They had to use drugs to calm her down before she went into cardiac arrest again."

It made sense that Esther hadn't wanted to talk about such a horrendous act in front of Jaci or Grace. But Pierce would have to face it with her. She'd need his strength and his support. She'd need someone to talk to who'd loved Charlie.

"Thanks for the info," Pierce said.

"It's not really a secret," Buck said. "Everyone

around here knows all about it. Mom feels real sorry for Esther. She says that all the time."

"I'm sure she does."

There was nothing left to say. Finding out Charlie was dead had been bad enough. But suicide? It made no sense at all. And now Esther's health was an issue, as well.

Pierce went back to the truck and drove away without speaking to Jaci or Grace. He had to have time to get his mind around this. His eyes watered and he was glad to be wearing sunglasses.

He didn't stop again until they reached the fishing hole where he'd spent many hours with Charlie, pulling bream and catfish out of the stocked, man-made pond, talking about life and how you couldn't give up no matter how hard life got.

Then the talk had been to encourage Pierce after the death of his parents. In the end, it was Charlie who had given up.

Pierce shifted the gear into Park. "This is it, the infamous fishing hole where I learned to bait a hook and catch bream and catfish."

Jaci put her game down, unbuckled her seat belt and jumped out of the backseat of his double-cab truck. She reached back inside for her fleece jacket, pulled it on and skipped around to the front of the truck.

"Look," she called, pointing to a group of half a dozen deer who were drinking from the pond. "I didn't know you had deer here, too."

"Deer and lots of other creatures," Pierce said. "All part of the adventure."

"Can we go fishing?"

"Not now. We don't have any poles or tackle with us. We'll come back and fish another day."

Pierce walked to the water's edge, picked up a small stone and skipped it across the surface of the pond.

Jaci picked up a stone and tried to copy him. Hers fell short of the water. "My rock can't dance."

"It takes practice," he said.

Two ducks flew in and landed on the water, a few yards from where they were standing. Jaci watched them, a fascinated gleam in her eyes until they flew away again.

"Did they fly away because the water is cold?"

"No, their feathers keep them warm. They were looking for food. I guess they didn't see anything that looked appetizing."

Jaci quickly moved on to the next thing that caught her eye. She climbed onto a wide stump and then jumped off. "Watch me, Grace," she called and then did the stunt over again.

"Wow. You are a good jumper." Grace walked over and stood next to Pierce. "Is anything wrong?" she asked, keeping her voice low enough not to grab Jaci's attention. "You've been awful quiet since you talked to Buck."

"It's…" He was about to say "nothing," except that

it wasn't nothing. It was haunting and troubling. And to be honest, he did want to talk to Grace about it.

"Buck said Charlie didn't die of natural causes. He shot himself in the head."

"An accident?"

"Suicide."

"Oh, no. Poor Esther. That must be so difficult. She loved him so much. I hope she doesn't blame herself in any way."

"Who knows? I need to hear the details from her. And there's more. Apparently, Esther found the body. The shock of that caused her to have a heart attack."

"She didn't mention having a heart attack. I wonder if she's following doctor's orders now. She was hauling in wood for the fireplace when she sprained her ankle."

"She can't run this ranch by herself. She couldn't do that even if her health was good. I've got to help. I'm just not sure where to start."

"How did you become so close to the Kavanaughs?"

"My parents were in a five-vehicle pileup on I-10 when I was fifteen. They were airlifted to a Houston hospital but pronounced dead on arrival. The 18-wheeler behind them literally peeled the top off the car."

"You must have been devastated."

"And scared. I was the oldest and I felt I had to be strong for my two younger brothers, who were twelve and fourteen."

"Did you have other family?"

"Yes, but we didn't know it at the time. Social services was going to split us up and put us in three different foster homes. We were all each other had and they were going to rip apart what little we had left of our family. I felt like I was the one letting my brothers down."

"Though you were only a kid yourself."

"I was, but I grew up pretty fast at that point. Anyway, the Kavanaughs heard about our plight and did enough finagling to take all three of us in."

"No wonder you feel so close to them."

"Right. We weren't just kids without a home to them. We were family, right from the first."

"I can understand that. Esther makes me feel like family and we just met. How long did you live with them?"

"Ten months. Then my mother's great uncle found out about us and contacted social services. Because he was actual kin, we were sent to live with him in Kansas."

"How did that go?"

"Uncle Raymond took some getting used to, but he was a good guy. He was retired but had coached high school football in his younger days, so our focus switched from ranching to football. We all played on the varsity team. My younger brother Tucker even went on to play a little college ball before deciding his real love was the rodeo."

"And you ended up a navy SEAL."

"And loved every minute of it. But it was Charlie

and Esther who were there for us when we needed them. It's too late for me to be here for Charlie, but I'll do whatever I can to help Esther. I wouldn't have it any other way."

Grace slipped her hand in his and squeezed. No words. Just touch. Exactly what he needed.

Pierce started to pull her into his arms for a hug but decided against it. She might misread the move. Or he might be misreading his own motive.

Paying more attention to his physical urges than to his brain was exactly how he'd ended up married to Leslie when they didn't really know each other.

He wouldn't make that mistake again, especially with a woman he already suspected of not being what she claimed.

PIERCE JOINED ESTHER and Grace in the family room. Esther was skimming through a ranch living magazine. Grace was standing next to the hearth, staring into the dancing flames as if they held answers to all the world's mysteries.

Pierce stretched out in Charlie's oversize leather recliner. He almost felt guilty sitting in it, but it had been a long day and the chair was just too damn inviting.

He'd been busy since they'd returned from the ranch tour. He'd repaired a couple of loose front porch steps, changed lightbulbs in the family room and kitchen overhead fixtures, fixed a leak in the kitchen sink. He'd even changed a battery in a chirping smoke detector.

The ranch was obviously not the only thing falling into a state of disrepair.

"Is Jaci asleep?" Esther asked.

"She's in bed," Pierce said. "That's all I can vouch for. I tried to read her a story, but she complained that I don't read it the way her mommy does."

"It's only natural she'd miss her mother," Esther said.

"I get that. I just think there was a better way of doing this."

"What was your idea?" Esther asked.

"That Leslie hang around at least a few more weeks. Give our daughter time to get to know me better and feel comfortable before her mother left the country."

Grace stepped away from the fire. "I should probably leave you two alone for this discussion. I'll be in my room if you need me."

"I'd rather you stay," Pierce said truthfully. "Jaci likes you, so you're definitely doing something right with her. I could use any pointers you want to share with me."

"You're better with her than you think, Pierce. It's clear you adore her. She's probably a little mad at you and her mother, but she's a smart and well-adjusted kid. She'll come around."

"What's so dang important in Cuba that Leslie couldn't wait a few weeks to leave?" Esther asked.

"My replacement. He's traveling there on business and she wants to go with him. I'm not worried about that. I just want my daughter to like me and not think I'm the bad guy."

"You're not the bad guy," Grace said. You're the father who took her to Texas on an adventure that she will never forget. Just be yourself and enjoy her. It's not going to take her long to come around."

"I'd like to have that in writing."

"You do know you're getting this parenting advice from a woman who's never had children?"

"Now you tell me."

"How long have you been divorced?" Grace asked.

"Two days," Pierce answered.

"That's all?"

"That's all it's been legal. We haven't been physically together in nine months. We haven't been emotionally together in longer than that."

"What about you, Grace?" Esther asked.

"Never married," she said. "At least not yet."

"You'll find the right man one day," Esther said. "When you do, grab him and hold on tight. That was Charlie's advice. He'd say you got to hold on to the things you love."

And that was probably as good a segue as Pierce was going to get.

"Charlie was a remarkable man," Pierce said. "I can't even imagine how hard his death must be on you. I wish you'd have gotten in touch with me or my brothers. At least one of us could have been here for you."

"I wasn't thinking too clearly at the time, but I

did finally leave a message at the last number I had for Riley. I figured that's why you showed up today."

"No. Riley never got the message."

"He's a rambler," Esther said. "In his blood, but I admit it's been really tough on me. It seems a little easier to bear with you, Jaci and Grace in the house now."

"About that," Pierce said, "how is your health since the heart attack—other than the sprained ankle?"

"How did you hear about the heart attack?"

"I ran into Buck Stalling today."

"I swear that boy's gonna be as big a gossiper as his mother. I'm fine. Can't do all the things Charlie did, but I'm making it."

"I'll help all I can while I'm here," Pierce offered. "I've never managed a ranch, but I'm sure Riley can give me lots of good advice."

"I'm not worried about the ranch," Esther said. "Ranch is nothing to me without Charlie. What I need is for you to help me find his killer."

Chapter Seven

Silvery moonlight filtered through the trees like fairy dust. The heavens sparkled with brilliant stars that appeared so close Grace felt she could have plucked them like crystal cherries.

Crickets and tree frogs serenaded. A cool breeze incited a riot of dry leaves escaping the hold of the ancient oak that stood as sentry over the sprawling ranch house.

The perfect haven—except that it wasn't.

Grace stood on the front porch, shivering in spite of the afghan pulled tightly around her shoulders. If Esther was right, the Double K Ranch was not immune to deadly evil.

Grace knew that kind of vicious, debased evil intimately. Had seen it in the eyes of her husband. Had heard it in his voice. Had sickened at the sight of it. Had fought it only to discover that the odds stacked against her were all but insurmountable.

The front door squeaked open. Footfalls sounded behind her. Even without turning, she knew that

Pierce had joined her. After only one day, she recognized the woodsy, musky scent of him. His presence had an uncanny, sensual effect on her.

Cold-blooded evil would be nothing new to him, either. He'd spent two tours of duty as a SEAL, going after an enemy that thrived on terror and recognized no moral boundaries.

Pierce crossed the porch and leaned against the support post mere inches from her.

"Do you think Esther is right about Charlie being murdered?" she asked.

"She's convinced of it," Pierce said.

"But you have your doubts?"

"Anything's possible, but as far as I know, Charlie didn't have an enemy in the world."

"Maybe it was a robbery gone bad," Grace suggested. "It's easy enough for a stranger to just walk onto the ranch without being noticed. I did it."

"But would a stranger stick around long enough to make it look like suicide? And it would have had to be a transient just passing through. No one who knew Charlie would go to the trouble to rob him. If you asked, he'd give you the shirt off his back and then throw in a pair of boots.

"Besides, she admitted to me just now that his wallet was still in his back pocket when they examined the body. Perhaps Esther simply can't face the fact that her beloved Charlie would willingly leave her.

"Running from reality doesn't sound like Esther. But like I said, anything's possible."

"What will you do?"

"A little investigating on my own. If I come to the same conclusion Esther did, then I'll do whatever I have to in order to get justice for Charlie. He'll likely chase me down from heaven with a lightning bolt if I do any less."

"If that's the case, he may have been trying to get your attention last night. I thought one had surely hit the house. We did lose power for a while."

"That was just a Texas welcome to check your mettle," Pierce said.

"That's what I thought the rooster was for."

"No, that was my welcome home," Pierce teased. "Haven't laughed that hard in years."

"You have a deranged sense of humor, Pierce Lawrence."

"So I've been told."

Somehow he'd managed to ease the tension on one level while increasing it on another. It was impossible to ignore the heated surge of attraction.

"I'm still not sure how Esther talked you into taking on the rooster."

"The same way she talked me into staying. She's such a dear, open and welcoming. Plus I couldn't really leave her alone to hobble around on that bad ankle. Of course, that was before I knew I'd have to fight off a rooster and steal eggs."

"And ride a horse," Pierce said. "Don't forget you're signed up for a lesson."

"Yeah, well, I'm going to have to take a rain check

on that, cowboy. Now that you and Jaci are here, there's really no point in my staying."

"What's the rush? Esther said you didn't have any immediate plans."

"I don't," she admitted. No one was ever waiting on her. "This is your and Jaci's special time with Esther. I'd only be in the way."

Pierce stepped closer and she met his gaze. His eyes looked smoky in the moonlight. Penetrating. Unsettling. She looked away as a choking need swelled inside her.

"What are you running from, Grace?"

"Nothing." Tension ridged her nerves. She struggled to stay calm and keep her voice steady. "Where did you get an idea like that?"

Pierce trailed the fingers of his right hand along her cheekbone and then eased them under the edge of her wig. "The fake hair. The oversize, dark-rimmed glasses that keep sliding down your nose. Ill-fitting clothes."

"I'm not into my appearance and the wig is more convenient than constantly dealing with my long hair."

"If you're trying to go unnoticed, Grace, it's not working."

His tone had become far too seductive. She had to get away from him before she said things she'd be sorry for. Before she started believing she could actually confide in him.

She couldn't. Pierce wouldn't rat her out. He was

one of the good guys. Brave, a lifesaver with the medals to prove it. That was the problem. If he knew the truth, he'd feel he had to save her the way he had to find justice for Charlie.

Only, trying to save Grace would put him and possibly even Jaci and Esther in danger.

"If you're in trouble, I can help," Pierce said.

Grace took a deep breath and pulled one of her rehearsed stories from her repertoire. "If you must know, I didn't lose my job. I had a bad breakup with an ex. I took all of his possessions he'd left at my place and dumped them into the nearest trash bin. I decided to take a short vacation while he cools down."

"Remind me not to make you mad."

"The guy deserved it and he knows it," she quipped. "As soon as he cools down, he'll be begging me to forgive him and take him back."

"You have to hang out somewhere until then. What better place than the Double K Ranch? Sounds like a win-win for all of us, the way I look at it."

Sounded like she'd backed herself into a corner and she suspected that Pierce hadn't actually bought her fabricated story.

"I'm really not needed here," she insisted.

"That's not true."

He reached over and took both her hands in his. The touch sent her emotions on a dangerous spiral. She couldn't give in to the desire that sparked inside her. A relationship with Pierce had nowhere to go. It would cause her to make bad decisions. Any kind of relationship would put her and Pierce in danger. It was a risk she could never take.

"We all need you here, Grace."

"I don't see why."

"Then you are underestimating yourself. Esther will likely be hobbling around for another day or two, possibly longer if you're not here to keep her from doing too much."

He inched closer. Her pulse skyrocketed.

"Jaci adores you," he continued. "And your being here with them while I'm off investigating the murder claim and taking care of some needed repairs around the ranch would make it a lot easier on me."

A few more days. Time with Pierce, Esther and Jaci that would make it all the more painful to go back to her safe little world of emotional isolation when this was over.

Pierce placed a thumb under her chin and tilted her face until his lips were only a hairbreadth away. "I want you to stay, Grace, because I really like having you here."

His lips touched hers. A longing struck full force, a need so intense she had to struggle to breathe.

She should turn and run. Her mind insisted. Her body refused to obey. She melted into the thrill of his kiss. Passion claimed her completely as he ravished her lips, pulling her closer until she felt the hard need of his desire pressing against her.

She wanted him. All the way. Right here. Right now.

The insanity of that finally knocked her back to

her senses. She pulled away, but her knees buckled and she would have crumpled into a heap at his feet if he hadn't held her up.

She struggled for something to say—anything that wouldn't let him know how intensely the kiss had affected her.

"I'll think about it," she muttered, her words barely coherent.

And then she turned and walked away quickly before she wound up back in his arms. Another kiss and all the reasons why she shouldn't get involved with Pierce might vanish completely.

THE CROWING OF a time-challenged rooster woke Pierce before sunrise made a dent in the gloomy gray of predawn. He jerked to full wakefulness instantly. SEAL training did that for a man.

This time there was no immediate physical threat, so his mind played a dirty trick on him, hurling him right back in the vat of troubled thoughts that had kept him awake the first half of the night.

Why in hell had he kissed Grace last night, aside from the fact that he'd been thinking about it from the first time he'd seen her hysterically fleeing the rooster?

Not that the kiss hadn't knocked him senseless. It most definitely had. And judging from the way Grace had kissed him back, she'd felt a bit of the magic, too.

That was precisely the problem.

It had instantly changed all the rules of engagement between him and Grace. They'd crossed a line, physically acknowledged the attraction that sizzled between them. Now casual touch or conversation would be practically impossible.

His life was a mess. His divorce from a woman he hadn't had a meaningful relationship with in years was barely final. He was trying to bond with a daughter when he knew absolutely nothing about parenting.

The last thing he needed was to fall for a woman who hadn't leveled with him about anything, possibly even her name.

Pierce kicked off the warm quilt, threw his legs over the side of the bed and padded to the bathroom. He took care of business, then washed his hands and splashed his face with cold water.

He'd love a cup of coffee but didn't want to risk waking Esther. With her ankle injury and the emotional turmoil she'd faced over the past three months, the rest would do her good.

Her claims of murder were as perplexing as they were worrisome. Yet it was equally hard to believe Charlie chose to end his life with a bullet to the head, leaving his cherished Esther to find his body.

Pierce hoped to meet with the sheriff today and get a few questions answered. After that, he'd have a better handle on where to go next with his own investigation.

Even more urgent, he needed to spend quality time with Jaci, horseback riding for certain. Four-wheeling over to Winding Creek would probably be fun for her, too. Of course, Jaci might only go with him if Grace came along.

Exploring the ranch with Grace. A flash of desire struck hard. He stifled a curse. The unwanted sensual stirrings were clearly not going down easy.

He picked up his laptop on the way back to bed. In minutes he'd pulled up countless links to people named Grace Addison.

A florist in Alabama. A songwriter in Wyoming. A web designer in California. A housewife blogger in New Mexico. An architect in Kansas. A few possibilities even in the Houston area, where she claimed she'd been working.

None of the candidates resembled his Grace in any way except gender. If Grace Addison was her real name, she'd done an excellent job of avoiding social media.

This was getting him nowhere fast. Pierce went in another direction. He looked up the contact information for Andy Malone, a former SEAL buddy who was currently a supervisor with the FBI and working in Florida.

It was too early to call even though Andy was on East Coast time. Pierce settled for a text asking Andy to give Pierce a call when he had a minute. In the meantime, Pierce needed more to go on if Malone was to be much help.

It struck him as he shut down the computer that kiss-and-call-the-FBI might be a much more serious offense in Grace's mind than kiss-and-tell.

GRACE STAYED IN the guest room until she no longer heard Pierce's deep voice wafting down the hall from the kitchen. The last thing she wanted to do this morning was face him across the breakfast table.

What could she possibly say to a stranger whose impromptu kiss had sent her over the moon?

"Pass the bacon" didn't seem to cover it.

"Your kiss was the most exciting thing that's happened to me in years, but getting involved with me is deadly."

Or perhaps "Everything you think you know about me is a lie"?

That would send most men running fast enough, but she couldn't count on that with Pierce. He was a medal-holding member of the navy SEALs, or at least he had been until recently. He'd be more likely to rush to her rescue than to run for the hills.

The amazing thing about all of this was that in spite of the ugly wig, unflattering eyeglasses and seeing her coated in mud, he'd actually wanted to kiss her.

He was right about one thing. The wig should go, at least for now. When she left the ranch, she'd dye her hair, but for now a haircut would have to do, hopefully one that would make her look significantly different from the hair-in-a-bun look she'd been wearing when her picture was snapped back in Tennessee.

Grace rummaged through the drawers of the dresser until she located a pair of shears that looked sharp enough to do the trick.

She stared into the big round mirror over the dresser. In her mind, she looked nothing like the eighteen-year-old student whose picture had been splashed all over the media six years ago.

The six years since then had hardened all her angles, stolen her innocence, cracked away at her youth.

Pulling a bouquet of hair strands between her fingers, she made the first cut. Dark brown hairs feathered to the top of the dresser and onto the floor, a few sticking to the front of her blue pullover sweater.

She had just made the third cut when someone tapped on her door. She was absolutely not ready to face Pierce like this. Fortunately, it was Jaci who burst in without waiting for an invitation.

"Good morning, Jaci."

"How come you slept so late?" Jaci asked.

"I've been awake a long time."

"You didn't get any pancakes."

"I wasn't hungry, so I read for a bit and then took a shower and got dressed."

Jaci climbed onto Grace's bed and let her legs dangle over the side. "Your hair looks funny."

Nothing like the honesty of a precocious five-year-old. "Hopefully, it will look better when I finish giving myself a haircut."

"I cut my hair once. Mommy made me go to time-out."

"I hope Esther doesn't do that to me."

Jaci giggled. "Grown-ups don't go to time-out."

"Whew. That's good to know."

"My mommy has blond hair."

"I'm sure she's very pretty."

"She is. She's not married to Daddy anymore."

"But I'm sure they'll both always love you."

"Mommy says Daddy just loves going to war."

"He's here with you now."

"We're on an adventure."

"Riding Dreamer yesterday looked like a very exciting adventure."

"I'm riding her again today. Daddy promised. Will you go with us?"

Not if she could help it. "We'll see, but you don't really need me there. Your daddy is the one who knows all about horses."

"You could learn."

"Let's just let you learn first."

"Okay. You can watch. Daddy's checking on cows right now, but when he gets back, we're going on another adventure."

"How exciting. I'm sure the two of you will have a great time."

"Not just two of us. All four of us." She held up four fingers to make her point. "You, Grandma Esther, Daddy and me."

"Are we all going to watch you ride Dreamer?"

"No. We're going for a ride in Daddy's truck."

"And where are we going on this great adventure?"

"Daddy has an appointment and we're going to get ice cream."

Grace had not agreed to field trips. Any kind of adventure with Pierce was risky. She'd avoided this kind of sensual temptation for years without problems.

But Pierce was different from anyone else she'd ever met. There was no way she could spend time around him and not fall even deeper under his spell.

GRACE MIGHT HAVE held her ground with Pierce, but with Esther and Jaci joining in the persuasion tactics, she didn't stand a chance. So just after the lunch dishes were cleared away, they all went trucking into the town of Winding Creek, looking far too much like the family they weren't.

Like the family she could never have no matter how badly she longed for one. Pierce stopped at a red light and then turned onto Main Street.

"So what do you think of our thriving metropolis?" Esther asked.

Grace looked down the narrow street that stretched in front of them. She gasped in amazement. "I feel like I've been dropped into the set of an old Western movie. The only thing missing is a gunfight."

"Thankfully the cops nowadays wouldn't put up with that," Esther said.

"But back in the day, there were plenty of bar fights and gunslingers around," Pierce assured her. "Winding Creek has quite an illustrious history if the town's old-timers can be believed."

"True or not, it looks the part." Always a lover of American history, Grace was mesmerized by this living preservation of the Old West. And to think she'd almost missed this the way she'd missed so much in her life. The price of staying alive.

Both sides of the narrow street were lined with one- and two-story weathered structures, many of the roofs made from uneven wooden shakes. A few of the storefronts appeared to have been reinforced with old brick. Huge pots of poinsettias or holiday greenery brightened the sidewalk.

Antique streetlights looked as if they should hold a candle instead of electric bulbs. Each one was decorated with fake greenery and a big silver star that was no doubt lit when the streetlights came on.

Every few yards there was a red painted bench, many occupied with an older man or two, likely waiting on their wives to finish shopping.

Jaci pressed her nose against the side window. "Where's the ice cream shop, Grandma? Daddy promised I could have a chocolate cone."

"In the next block. Blue Bell, made right here in Texas."

"And always larruping good," Pierce said.

"What's 'larruping good'?"

"That's how cowgirls say 'doggone fine' in Texas."

"Larruping." Jaci tried the word on for size. The syllables became twisted on her tongue, but she looked quite pleased with her new word.

Pierce was definitely making progress with winning her over, though Jaci had refused to let him brush her hair before they left the house and insisted

Grace do it. Grace suspected he was glad to get out of that.

But Jaci had also turned down his offer to go with him to put out some fresh hay and feed for the cattle even though he'd made it sound like fun. That had clearly disappointed him.

"There's a new bakery in town, too," Esther said. "Best sweets you ever put in your mouth, I swear. And almost too pretty to eat. Red velvet cupcakes that melt in your mouth. Lemon tarts. And kinds of cookies folks around Winding Creek have never even heard of."

"Larruping cookies," Jaci said and then giggled at her own cleverness.

"You got it, cowgirl," Pierce said.

"Can we get cookies, too?" Jaci asked.

"I think we can swing that, since you almost cleaned your plate at lunch. But then I've never known anyone who couldn't eat a couple of pieces of Esther's fried chicken."

"You ate more than two."

"I'm a growing boy."

Jaci giggled again. "Mommy would have said you'd get fat."

"Mommy might have been right. I'll go easy on the ice cream."

Grace found it amazing that Jaci was so well adjusted that her parents' split hadn't torn her apart. Of course, it must help that there was no open bitterness or animosity about the divorce, at least not on Pierce's part.

"See that sprawling two-story structure on the corner," Esther said. "That was the Cowman's Saloon back when the town was first settled. There are some wild tales about what happened in that place in the old days."

"I bet. What is it now?"

"Henry Logan's hardware store is on the first floor. He's a fixture in town, been in that one spot for as long as I can remember. Charges too much for his merchandise, though. I priced a porch swing last week that he had on display. The wood was beautiful but not worth the price he had on it."

"What happened to your porch swing?" Pierce asked.

"Blew off in a storm, hit a tree and busted into a hundred pieces. It was my fault. I'd taken it off the chains to repaint it."

"That must have been some storm to pick up a porch swing."

"Like a small tornado," she said. "'Bout tore the roof off the barn, but luckily didn't do any damage to the house. Praise the Lord for that. And look at that store on your left." Esther jumped to a new topic with hardly a breath in between. She clearly liked showing off the town to her guests.

"Creighton's Jewelry," Pierce said. "I remember that. I never shopped there, but I remember the name."

"Adler Creighton's famous now. Jake Dalton was

in the other day to buy a Christmas present for his new wife, the former Carolina Lambert. I heard that from Adler himself."

"Do you know everyone in town?" Grace asked.

"Pretty much everybody knows everyone inside the Winding Creek town limits, at least to speak to on the street. You keep running into the same people at church events, holiday celebrations and the Cattlemen's Association."

"Don't forget high school football games," Pierce reminded her. "You know how Texas is about its Friday night lights."

"What is the population of Winding Creek?" Grace asked.

"Twenty-two hundred at last count, but that probably includes a dog or two."

"It's hard to believe that few people can support all these shops," Grace said, checking out the windows of a gift shop with elaborate displays.

"That twenty-two hundred number doesn't include all the ranches scattered around the area outside the town limits nor the summer folks who have houses and cabins along Winding Creek."

"Nor all the tourists that drive out from San Antonio and Austin on nice weekends to go antiques shopping or just to escape the fast lane." Pierce pulled into an angled parking spot in front of a Western shop. He helped Esther and her cane out of the passenger side of the front seat. Grace and Jaci piled out of the back and stepped onto the curb.

An older model black compact car that was passing behind them slowed down, likely looking for a parking place. Esther put up a hand to wave. The driver looked away without waving back.

"Nosy old coot," Esther said. "Slow down to gawk and not even wave back."

"Who was that?" Pierce asked.

"I didn't get a good look at him, and I didn't recognize the car. You can bet he's not from around here. It's just the tourists who don't wave."

The car turned at the next corner.

"First stop, the Western shop," Pierce announced.

"Are we gonna buy more jeans?" Jaci asked.

"Not today. I need a good denim work jacket and some flannel shirts."

"While you get that, I'm going next door to get Jaci a pair of Christmas pajamas they had displayed in the window last week," Esther said. "I'll need you to come with me, Jaci, so we can make sure they fit."

"I'll be in the ladies' jeans department," Grace said.

She got sidelined by the boots before she made it to the jeans. She owned practical boots made for warmth and walking in the snow. The pair of boots that caught her eye and stopped her in her tracks was not practical.

They were stunning. Red with a black embroidered design running down the full length of them. She picked one up. The leather was incredibly soft.

A salesclerk walked up beside her. "Would you like to try them on?"

"How much are they?"

"Just 295 dollars. They're a really good buy at that price."

But not for a woman who would be leaving the ranch any day now.

"Just try them on," the salesclerk encouraged. "It doesn't cost to do that. What size do you wear?"

"A six."

"Good, I think I have those in a six. I'll be right back."

Trying them on was a terrible idea. The minute Grace slipped her feet in them, she knew she wouldn't be taking them off. A crazy waste of money, but she was doing a lot of crazy things since arriving in Texas.

Pierce showed up while she was paying for them.

"Wow. I love those. Red. You'll even excite the bulls."

A terrifying thought. "They wouldn't chase me, would they?"

"I was only kidding. Actually, bulls and other cattle are color-blind. It's the waving cape that gets their attention in a bullfight."

"Good to know. I'll be careful where I wave a cape."

Esther and Jaci were waiting when they walked outside. Both got excited over the boots. That felt good. The boots were her first splurge in years.

Jaci hopped and skipped ahead, eager to get to the ice cream store, but skidded to a stop before she made it. She pressed her nose to the window of the florist shop, hypnotized by the beautifully decorated Christmas tree.

At least seven feet tall. Silver and jeweled ornaments and shiny silver ribbons cascading from the top to the floor. Hundreds of tiny white lights sparkling through the green branches.

"That's the mostest prettiest tree I ever saw," Jaci announced.

"It is beautiful," Grace agreed.

"Is it for sale?" Jaci asked.

"I reckon it is," Esther said as she and Pierce joined them. "Everything's for sale if you have enough money, but we don't need to buy a tree. We have acres of them. Your daddy and his brothers picked out the most perfect tree I ever laid my eyes on the Christmas they lived on the Double K."

"I remember that tree," Pierce said. "We could barely haul it home in the back of the pickup truck. Charlie said it was never going to fit in the house."

"Did it fit?" Jaci asked.

"After we cut about a foot off."

"And you boys decorated it with wooden angels you made out in Charlie's workshop," Esther added.

"That's right. Tucker insisted on painting the wings on his angels blue. Wonder what ever happened to those."

"I still have them, hang them on the tree every year, even the one your dog chewed the head off of."

"Where's your dog now?" Jaci asked excitedly.

"He died years ago, but don't worry. He lived a nice long life."

"Can we get a dog?"

"One thing at a time," Pierce said. "First we should get a Christmas tree, that is if you'll help me pick out the right one."

"I want a tall one that reaches to the top of your hat," Jaci said.

"I know just the spot in the family room for it," Esther said. "It's where Charlie put our tree every year."

Yesterday Esther had considered avoiding Christmas. Apparently, having Pierce and Jaci around had changed her mind. Now she sounded almost as excited as Jaci. Grace suspected this made her feel she was honoring Charlie as well as making Jaci happy.

"I have a lot of ornaments," Esther added, "but if we had some of those silver teardrop-shaped ones on that tree in the window, I think it would be our most beautiful Christmas tree ever."

New traditions added to the old. A tree with handmade angels and memories. A family Christmas.

A lump formed in Grace's throat. For the past six years she'd made it through the holidays by keeping her expectations low and feeling sorry for herself at a minimum. By not thinking of family, not aching for what she'd never have again.

Christmas at the Double K Ranch would be the ultimate reminder of all she'd lost.

But Esther, Jaci and Pierce desperately needed a little Christmas.

Esther, who'd been drowning in grief. Jaci, who missed her mother and was wary of her relationship with a father she was slowly getting used to. Pierce, who'd spent eight years fighting terrorists in a hellhole on the other side of the world and had come home to face a divorce.

They needed the tree, the decorations, the lights and the joy. There was no way Grace could steal that from them. So she'd act as thrilled as they did and silently make plans to spend Christmas anywhere but there.

The four of them marched inside the store and Esther and Jaci examined the silver ornaments, oohing and aahing at each one. Pierce put a hand on the small of Grace's back and guided her to a display of miniature Santas, just out of Jaci's earshot.

"What's wrong?" he asked. "You look like Santa left coal in your stocking."

"I'm fine. I do feel a little like an outsider here, the stray that wandered up but doesn't quite fit."

"I get that, but we're all kind of strays here. Even misfits need a little Christmas—and maybe some mistletoe," he teased.

The heated zing danced through her again. No way could she start thinking of mistletoe and kisses and think straight.

"I didn't get to tell you how gorgeous you look today. Please throw that wig away."

"Don't you have an appointment about now?"

Pierce pushed up the sleeve of his pullover sweater

and checked his watch. "Actually, I'm meeting with the local sheriff in ten minutes, but it's only a short drive from here. How do you feel about going with me?"

"Then I'd really be in the way."

"You could be a help. You didn't know Charlie, so you could get an unbiased take on what Sheriff Cavazos has to say about the suicide."

She felt a quick wave of panic at the thought. Her stomach knotted. The last person she wanted to talk to was the sheriff. If anyone was going to recognize her, it would likely be someone who'd been in law enforcement six years ago.

"I'd be really uncomfortable in that situation. Besides, I promised Jaci I'd go for ice cream with her."

"It was just a thought," Pierce said. "I didn't mean to upset you."

"You didn't." But of course he knew that he had. She'd felt so shaky inside it must have shown in her reaction.

"Enjoy the ice cream and the town," Pierce said. "I'll give you a call when I leave the sheriff's office and we can all meet back here at the truck."

"Okay. Good luck."

"Thanks. I just hope I get enough information to form a reasonable opinion on how Charlie died."

"Me, too."

Grace watched Pierce walk away. He might have just finished two tours of duty as a navy SEAL, but he looked one hundred percent cowboy right down to the great swagger.

For the first time in years, she'd met a man she'd really like to get to know better. A man who made her laugh and made her feel safe even when she knew safety was impossible. A man whose kiss had thrilled her to the core.

A man with a daughter, which made any kind of relationship with him even more troublesome. She would never risk Jaci's safety.

Suddenly finding it difficult to breathe, she wiggled out of her red fleece jacket. When that didn't help, she walked outside to wait for Esther and Jaci to finish paying for their armload of purchases.

She managed to pull herself together by the time Esther and Jaci stepped out the door. Jaci rushed over and grabbed Grace's hand. "We got silver reindeer and balls with jewels on them and tiny silver slippers like Cinderella wears. Do you want to see them?"

"Definitely, but I can wait until we get home. If we start pulling them out here on the street, we might drop one and break it."

"Oh, no!" Jaci exclaimed. "We might break the silver slippers. I like them best. They sparkle."

"Oh, goody," Grace said. "I love sparkly things."

"Can we get ice cream now?" Jaci asked.

"Best idea I've heard all day," Esther agreed.

Jaci skipped ahead. Knowing Esther couldn't keep up, Grace hurried to catch up with the energetic preschooler. They were only a few steps from the door to the ice cream shop when Grace heard the squeal of tires.

She spotted the source immediately. A black car swerved around the corner at breakneck speed. What kind of idiot would drive that fast on this narrow, busy street?

Esther put up her hand and shook her fist at the reckless driver. The car slowed just before it was even with them. Instinctively, Grace checked out the driver. He stuck out his hand and she spotted the gleam of sunshine on metal.

Her survival instincts checked in.

"Get down," she screamed. Impulsively, she threw her jacket over Jaci's head and took her down to the sidewalk, covering Jaci's body with her own.

Three blasts. Quick. Loud. The crash of shattering glass. Then screams. Grace wasn't sure whose— possibly hers.

Glass rained down on top of her. Warm blood trickled down her face. The horrors closed in on her like the blackest night. One of Tom's hatchet men had found her again.

Chapter Eight

Pierce was stopped at a pedestrian crossing two blocks away from the ice cream shop, windows down in his truck, George Strait on the radio, his mind on Grace.

She'd wowed him yesterday in a hideous wig, baggy jeans and unflattering glasses. Today she was so adorable it was hard not to get turned on just looking at her.

Gorgeous sun-tipped brown hair that tumbled in loose curls around her shoulders. Jeans that actually fit her cute behind. No makeup except maybe a shimmer of blush on her cheeks. Natural eyebrows that emphasized her seductive, brandy-colored eyes.

He knew he wasn't in the right place in his life to kindle a new relationship. Problem was, he was already feeling the heat.

A crashing explosion of noise brought him slamming back to reality. Rapid gunfire. In a second he was back in the war zone, death slashing the very air he breathed.

Muscles taut, threaded like fine steel. His mind razor sharp. Adrenaline rushing like a flood-swollen river.

But he wasn't in a war zone. He was in Winding Creek, Texas, probably the safest place in the universe.

And then he heard the high-pitched screams and calls for help. He swerved into a U-turn and shoved the accelerator to the floor. Even before he reached the corner near the ice cream shop, he saw a cluster of people huddled near the door.

Esther was there, holding on to the arm of a woman he didn't recognize. There was no sign of Jaci or Grace. The parking spaces were taken. He left his truck in the middle of the road and bolted toward the crowd.

Finally, he spotted Grace, sitting on the sidewalk, scrunched up against the storefront. Blood stained her cheek and dripped from her chin. Her arms were wrapped around Jaci and she was rocking her back and forth to comfort her. The large display window above them was shattered.

"Someone call an ambulance." Pierce pushed through the bystanders and knelt beside Grace. "Are you two okay?"

All Grace managed was a nod, her face ghostly white, her hands trembling.

"You're bleeding from your right temple," Pierce said.

"It's nothing," she assured him. "Just make sure Jaci's okay."

"My elbow hurts," Jaci said.

Pierce peeled off her light jacket and Jaci pointed at a red patch of flesh, but the skin wasn't broken.

Everyone was safe. Pierce's breathing steadied.

Esther leaned over Jaci for a look at the elbow. "Must have gotten that when you hit the sidewalk. I'll bet a chocolate ice cream cone will fix that right up."

Pierce took a clean white handkerchief from his pocket and held it against the oozing blood at Grace's temple. Thankfully, the cut wasn't deep, but it was an inch or more in length.

Jaci pushed her lips into a pout and touched her elbow. "I want Mommy."

"I know, sweetheart."

"I want to go home."

He doubted she was talking about the Double K Ranch. More likely, she was referring to the rented apartment she'd shared with Leslie, a home that didn't actually exist anymore.

Pierce reached out to Grace and helped her up and back into her jacket. He tried to lift Jaci into his arms, for himself as much as her. He'd come far too close to losing her.

She pushed away from him and put her arms around Grace's waist. At least there was someone his daughter trusted.

He took a good look at the bullet holes in the shattered window. "What happened?"

The bystanders' chatter he'd managed to ignore

up to this point grew louder. Everyone talked at once until Esther shut them up.

"Pierce can't understand a word you say when you all squawk at once. I was standing right here. I saw everything and I'll do the talking."

A take-charge woman. That was the Esther he remembered.

"Some jackass in a black car came round the corner like he was hightailing it from the devil. He slowed down just long enough to poke a gun out the window and start firing. Might have been the same guy gawking at us earlier, but it happened too fast for me to be sure."

"That's what happened, all right," some guy added.

Others all spoke up, a bit more orderly this time.

"A random shooting right here on Main Street. We're not putting up with that."

"I heard someone yell 'Take cover.' A split-second later bullets started flying."

"Grace did the yelling," Esther said, "and then she grabbed Jaci and fell down right on top of her."

"That's what saved the kid," someone attested.

"Saved both of them," Esther said. "Those bullets hit right where Grace and Jaci had been standing."

A police car pulled up and stopped right behind Pierce's truck. Hand on the butt of his gun, a deputy scanned the group as he sauntered over to the curb.

"Someone want to tell me what's going on here?"

They all told him at once.

"Did anyone get a license number?" the deputy asked.

No one had.

By the time the deputy got around to questioning Grace, she was standing next to Pierce and Esther, Jaci holding on to Grace's leg, half-hidden behind it.

His daughter, but he hadn't been the one to save her. Grace had. Two days ago, he hadn't even known Grace. Now she was a vital part of his life, the fast-thinking heroine who'd saved his daughter's life.

Grace repeated the same scenario to the deputy as Pierce had heard from her and Esther. The deputy asked for details that she couldn't supply, but he didn't push too hard. No doubt the shooting had shaken him up, too.

The deputy took Grace's contact information including that she was visiting the Double K Ranch. "There's an ambulance on the way," he assured her.

"All I have is a little cut," Grace protested. "I'm not getting into an ambulance."

"That's up to you," the deputy said. "But the requirements are that once the ambulance is here, you have to sign a release if you don't want medical attention."

"Fine."

"Not totally fine," Pierce said. "That cut could probably use a few stitches."

"There's a local emergency medical clinic out on the highway, just down from the new HEB market," Esther said. "Ellen Crosby's son is the physician in charge. You remember him, Pierce. He played varsity football with you."

"I remember him," Pierce said, not really interested in talking old times right now. "I'll see that Grace gets the wound checked out."

Even if they had to drive all the way to San Antonio to do it.

"I'll hang around here until our crime scene investigators get here to take a few pictures," the deputy said. "If you and the girl need a ride home, Mrs. Kavanaugh, I can call another deputy to drive y'all back to the ranch."

"I'll give them a ride home," the woman standing next to Esther offered. "Not out of my way at all. After we get Jaci her ice cream, of course."

Pierce had forgotten how friendly Winding Creek was, which made a random shooting in the middle of the day even more bizarre.

"I'm sure Sheriff Cavazos or one of the department's investigators will get in touch with you before the day is over, Miss Addison."

"I've told you all I know and it's the same as everyone else told you. There's really no use for anyone from your department to waste time questioning me further."

"It's just part of the investigation process. We don't tolerate crime in these parts. A random shooting on Main Street in Winding Creek is serious, and I guarantee you it will be treated that way."

"Just arrest the lunatic who did it," Esther said.

"We will. You can be sure of that."

Pierce was far from convinced this had been a random shooting. He'd thought from the beginning Grace was running from someone or something. That person or thing might have just caught up with her and could have killed both her and Jaci.

It was time for him to get some real answers about the mystery woman whose kiss blew his mind and whom his daughter was growing increasingly attached to.

He would not take any chances with his daughter's life. As things stood right now, Grace had just saved Jaci's life. Those two facts intricately bound them no matter where they went from here.

"I THINK THIS should heal nicely and not give you any trouble. I'd like to see you again in four days, sooner if it shows signs of infection."

"Okay," Grace agreed to the young doctor's orders, knowing she'd be long gone from Texas in four days."

"You're lucky we're only looking at a small cut. From what I heard, if you hadn't hit the ground when you did, you'd likely be fighting for your life right now."

Or dead. She felt a cold shiver deep inside her bones, the fear not so much for herself as for Jaci and Esther. They would never have been in that situation if not for her.

The sheriff and the rest of the town might believe the shooting was random. Grace knew better.

You will be looking over your shoulder for the rest

*of your life, always wary, expecting the worst. And
one day it will find you.*

At eighteen, the full impact of the attorney's warning hadn't fully sunk in. Even if it had, she would
have made the same choice.

She'd let her attraction for Pierce and her desire
to be part of a family lure her into making the wrong
choice now. Had she left this morning, none of this
would have happened. Pierce thought she'd saved
Jaci's life.

How would he feel if he knew the attack had been
specifically directed at Grace? Or had he come to that
conclusion on his own?

Doctor Crosby finished his spiel, but her mind had
already moved on. Now if she could just get through
the rest of the day without being bombarded with
questions from law enforcement.

Extensive questioning or investigation would almost guarantee that sooner or later someone would
recognize her. It would make the news and make disappearing again that much more difficult.

She had to get out of town fast before anyone connected her with her nightmarish past. All she had to
do was avoid the sheriff or one of his detectives until
she could disappear again.

Unfortunately, that proved to be wishful thinking.

Chapter Nine

Sheriff Cavazos had suggested Pierce and Grace meet him at a coffee shop near the clinic. Pierce hadn't met him before but quickly spotted the khaki-uniformed lawman sitting at a booth in the back of the restaurant.

The sheriff waved them back, apparently recognizing them from the pictures taken by the deputy at the crime scene. Pierce was certain they would have talked at length by now.

Grace scooted into the booth opposite the sheriff. Pierce slid in beside her. No sooner had she sat down than she started rubbing a spot on her neck just below her right ear.

"Sorry about this afternoon, Grace," the sheriff said when they'd taken care of introductions. "Getting shot at is a helluva Winding Creek welcome. Too bad you got such an unfavorable impression of our usually friendly little town."

"I didn't. These things happen. The people in town couldn't have been more supportive."

"Good to hear that. But things like that don't happen

here, and I don't plan to let them get started, either—not as long as I'm wearing this." He tapped a fingertip against the bronze badge on his shirt.

"Fortunately, there were no serious injuries," Grace said.

"Yeah, but there could've been a bloodbath out there. Women, kids. Grown men with guns. No telling what might have happened if it hadn't been over and done with so fast. As it was, you got wounded from broken glass."

"Nothing to deny about any of that," Pierce agreed.

A middle-aged waitress with a warm smile and a twangy voice came by, refilled the sheriff's coffee mug and took their orders. Coffee, black for Pierce, with cream for Grace.

The sheriff sipped his coffee and then pulled a small black notebook from his shirt pocket and placed it on the table. "I hate to bother you with more questions, but I need some additional information for my records."

"I told your deputy all I know."

"He said you were mighty cooperative. I appreciate that. Your quick action impressed the hell out of him, yelling at people to get down and then throwing yourself on top of the kid."

"I saw the gun. The rest was all reflexes."

"Good reflexes. Did you ever work in law enforcement?"

"No."

"Then I'll bet you're a good athlete."

"Not particularly."

"What do you do for a living?"

Grace looked down at her hands and hesitated before answering. "I was an office manager in my last job."

"What do you do now?"

"I'm currently unemployed. There have been a lot of layoffs in Houston since the price of crude oil plunged."

"Yep. Hurting folks all over the state. So you're just visiting Esther between jobs?"

"I'm passing through. Esther sprained her ankle, so I stayed a few days to help out."

Grace hadn't exactly lied, but she had made it seem that she and Esther had been friends before the sprained ankle. Pierce knew now that wasn't the case.

The waitress showed up with their coffees and Sheriff Cavazos waited until she was out of earshot before continuing. "Did you get a good look at the shooter?"

"No. I explained all that to your deputy. The car was speeding down the street. All I saw was the weapon."

"And you're not certain if this was the same car you'd seen a few minutes earlier on the street."

"They were both black. That's really all I know."

The sheriff took a pen from his pocket and clicked it. "I'll need your full name—for the records."

Again she hesitated and reached for her coffee,

sipping slow before answering. "Grace Ann Addison," she said, her voice low and her gaze downcast.

"Can I see your driver's license?"

She spread her hands palm down on the table. "I don't have it with me."

"Where is it?"

"It's back at the Double K Ranch, in the glove compartment of my car. I wasn't driving today, so I didn't think I'd need it."

"No problem. I can get that from you later. I do need your permanent address and your social security number."

"I don't actually have a current home address. I'm relocating from Houston to Albuquerque."

"I see. Then give me your social security number and a phone number where I can reach you."

She rattled off the numbers.

Cavazos took another sip of coffee and wiped his mouth on a paper napkin. "At least the timing was good for your visit to Esther. She's had a real rough time of it since Charlie died. It hit her hard. She's starting to concoct and believe crazy conspiracy theories."

"Esther is still grieving, but she seems perfectly sane to me," Grace said.

"I assume you're talking about her thinking Charlie was murdered and that nothing's being done about it," Pierce said. "That's what I had planned to talk to you about before the shooting canceled our appointment."

"I was afraid of that," Cavazos said. "Esther keeps hammering away at the murder theory, but I oversaw the investigation myself. There wasn't a smidgen of evidence to support murder."

"I'd like to read the evidence report."

"No problem. Then hopefully you can talk some sense into Esther."

"I'll do what I can," Pierce said, "but to tell you the truth, I'm having a difficult time believing Charlie would kill himself."

"Maybe that's because you haven't seen him in quite a few years. The last time you actually spent any extended time with him, you were a teenager."

"Did you investigate me, too?"

"You and your brothers' names came up during the investigation. We weren't able to get in touch with any of you."

"I was serving in the military in the Middle East."

"So I heard. I questioned dozens of people myself," the sheriff said. "No one ever had a bad word to say about Charlie Kavanaugh. He was a good church-goer. The first man on the scene if someone needed a helping hand. He wasn't robbed. Esther didn't kill him. There's no motive for murder."

"So where's the motive for him to commit suicide?" Pierce asked.

"He was having some money problems. That drought a couple of years back was hard on all the ranchers. They couldn't grow enough hay and crops to feed the cattle. Charlie sold off at least a hundred head and took a big loss. No one was paying a decent price for beef then."

"I'm sure his friend Dudley Miles would have backed him for a year or two if it was that bad."

"Guess you haven't heard about Dudley." The sheriff finished off his coffee and reached for his wallet, obviously ready to end this conversation.

"Heard what?" Pierce asked.

"Dudley has his own problems, serious ones."

"How serious?"

"He's doing time."

"Are you saying Dudley Miles is behind bars?"

"Yep. In prison for the next ten years before he can even request parole."

Now Pierce was doubly shocked. Dudley Miles was a longtime friend of Charlie's and owned and operated one of the largest and most successful ranches in this part of the state.

"It's a long story," Cavazos said, "but it involved that troublemaking daughter of his. Get Esther to give you the details. Get me started on that mess and I can go on for hours and I don't have time for that today."

Cavazos pulled his phone from his pocket. "I've got an important call coming in. I'll need to take it in private. You two enjoy your coffee. It's on me."

The sheriff told the caller to hold on a second, time he used to put down enough cash to cover the tab.

The waitress stopped by and refilled their cups. "Fresh pot. Can I get you two anything else? Best apple pie in Texas."

They both declined. Grace sipped her coffee. Her

hands shook, not so much she spilled the hot liquid, but enough that Pierce noticed.

"Are you okay?" he asked.

"As okay as you'd expect after a random shooting, a few stitches in my head and talk of suicide and prison."

"Nothing like Texas when you need an adventure."

"It's you and Jaci who are looking for adventure. Not me."

Surprisingly, the sheriff rejoined them before they finished their second cup of coffee. He didn't sit down.

"Good news."

"We can use some of that," Pierce said.

"One of the men sitting on the bench across the street from the florist shop when the shooting took place recognized the shooter."

"A local?" Pierce asked.

"Not currently. Name's Reid Peterson. Young guy. In his early twenties. Reportedly a member of a drug gang in San Antonio and probably so high on crack cocaine he didn't even know where he was."

Hard for Pierce to imagine a guy like that was targeting Grace, so just maybe the shooting was random. "What was this San Antonio drug member doing in Winding Creek?"

"His parents have a truck farm out on Blackstone Road. He must have been visiting them."

"Is this his first time to cause this kind of trouble?"

Alarm had crept into Grace's voice. Pierce reached over and took one of her hands in his. It was icy cold.

"First time he's done a drive-by in Winding Creek,

but he was arrested on vandalism charges several times when he was in high school. Shot out all the windows in the house of a schoolmate he'd gotten in a fight with after football practice."

"Probably on drugs even then," Pierce said.

"No doubt, but hopefully he'll get the rehab he needs behind bars."

"Then you are definitely convinced today's shooting was random?" Grace asked.

"Absolutely. Crack cocaine can really mess up a person's mind."

"I've heard that."

Her exhale became a sigh, as if she'd been holding her breath. Hearing that the sheriff was convinced the shooting was random was obviously a relief to her. As far as Pierce was concerned, that indicated that she suspected she'd been intentionally targeted.

Pierce was more convinced than ever that she was running scared. Today's shooting might have nothing to do with it, but then again it could. She might not want his help, but no way was he going to let her take off on her own again until he was sure she was safe.

Short of calf roping her and tying her down, he had no idea how he was going to accomplish that.

Thanks to Charlie, he was right handy with a calf rope.

GRACE STARED OUT the window at rolling hills, cattle grazing lazily in green pastures, and mile after mile of barbwire fences. The tension that had scraped along her nerve endings when talking to the sheriff had eased but not completely melted away.

The events of the day had left her drained, more from the emotional trauma than the physical. If she'd brought danger to Jaci or Esther, she wouldn't have been able to live with herself. She knew that torment all too well—all part of the never-ending nightmare that ruled her life.

The sweet relief she'd experienced when the sheriff assured her the shooting was definitely random had been quickly laced with anxiety. As much as she wanted to believe Cavazos was right, she could not rule out that those bullets had been meant for her.

The stalker from Tennessee could have tracked her to this area. She didn't see how, but it was possible. And once he did, the Lacoste family likely still had connections in drug trafficking that could encompass the drug gangs in San Antonio.

Or the years of loneliness and personal detachment may have shaped her into a paranoid fruitcake. The man in Tennessee might have been just what he claimed, a man whose job had brought him to Mountain Edge.

For all she knew, he could have been a photographer capturing the magic of the quaint mountain community on film, including the homely librarian's assistant with her hair in a bun, a skirt that was too long and sensible shoes.

Pierce turned onto a narrow dirt road that seemed to disappear into a strand of pine trees so tall and thick it completely hid the sun.

"Where are we going?"

"Back to the ranch."

The truck bounced and jerked through and around a maze of deep holes on a road in even worse shape than the logging road she'd stopped to explore two days ago.

Only two days and yet she felt as if she were being devoured by this lifestyle.

Pierce swerved to miss a large rock that had somehow ended up in the middle of the road.

"You're going to ruin your tires and shocks," she said.

"The salesman assured me this truck could take whatever I dished out. If it can't handle this, I'm taking it back."

"If you can get it back to the dealer in one piece."

"You're not too delicate for a few bumps, are you?"

"This is a few bumps about like the Grand Canyon is a small gully."

Pierce stopped the truck at a metal gate. "The road gets a little better after this."

"Are you sure? You've been gone from the area a long time."

"Yes, but I followed this road yesterday and discovered a woman playing chase with a rooster."

"Very funny. Then this is the back entrance to the Double K Ranch?"

"Yep."

"There's no sign. How do visitors know where they are?"

"Charlie didn't build it for visitors. He built it so he could haul feed to this part of the ranch in the spring when some of his other ranch roads flooded."

Grace twisted in her seat so she could get a better look. "Nothing looks familiar. Which way is the house or the big barn near the chicken coop?"

"They're off to the east, over several hills and a creek or two."

She opened the truck door. "I'll get the gate. What's the code for the lock, or do you have a key?"

"No key. No code. It's never locked."

"Then what's the point of the gate?"

"Same as the cattle gap. To keep the livestock in."

Grace climbed from the truck, unlatched the gate and swung it open. Once Pierce had driven through, she walked across the cattle gap. No use to be careful of her beautiful red boots. They'd been cut by shattered glass, too.

Grace couldn't imagine living in an isolated place like this and not bothering to lock gates. She'd never sleep. Yet Esther didn't lock her house during the day even though she was convinced someone had come onto the ranch and murdered her husband.

"We should call Esther," she said as she got back in the truck. "She's surely wondering when we'll be back."

"I gave her a call while you used the restroom

back at the coffee shop and told her we were taking the scenic route home."

"How was Jaci?"

"Fine, I assume. She had her hands buried in sugar cookie dough, so I didn't actually get to talk to her."

The road turned east in the direction where Pierce had said the house was. He turned west, then gunned the engine as the altitude climbed. The truck bumped along the hard earth with Pierce swerving often to avoid running into a tree or bush.

Once over that hill, they stopped at a second gate. Again, she jumped out and did gate duties.

"How many gates does a ranch need?" she asked when they were moving again.

"Sometimes dozens," Pierce said, "depending on the size of the ranch. If you didn't have them, all the pastures would run together. You couldn't control your grazing patterns. Running a ranch is more than just throwing out a little hay every now and then."

"You learned all that in the ten months you were living with the Kavanaughs?"

"Yeah. My brothers and I did our fair share of baling hay, cleaning out the horse stalls, fixing fences, helping with roundups and branding, giving routine injections and most everything else that has to be done around the ranch."

"The exciting life of a cowboy."

"Not always exciting, but I sure learned to get comfortable in my own skin here and developed a real love for the land. The only part I didn't like was turning bulls into steers, but I became really good at it."

"That's high on the list of things I never want to watch you do."

"That's no way for a cowgirl to talk. We're going to have to get you on a horse to get you in the spirit."

"I should tell you now, that isn't going to happen."

"Why not?"

"They are too big and I didn't see brakes, steering wheels or seat belts to them."

"After a few times in the saddle, you'll love the feeling of freedom and be glad you're not buckled into anything."

She shook her head. "You are never convincing me of that."

He reached across the seat and let his hand rest on her shoulder. "Never underestimate a cowboy's power of persuasion."

That, she wouldn't do. Every minute she spent around Pierce, the deeper he crawled under her skin. When he touched her the way he was now, she could feel the heat of desire from her head to her toes.

"When I was younger, I planned to own a ranch like this myself one day," Pierce said. "Only my second day back on the Double K and I'm leaning that way again. Once the cowboy lifestyle gets into your blood, it's hard to leave it."

"And yet you chose to become a navy SEAL."

"That got into my blood, too. Maybe it's the idea of

being tied down to a nine-to-five job in a suffocating office that I can't get into."

Grace could believe that about Pierce. He had a free spirit about him that she envied. Perhaps that was part of the reason she found him so exciting. But not the only reason.

He was different from any man she'd ever met. Ruggedly handsome. All man but with that cocky boyishly exciting manner that made her feel at ease even when she knew she shouldn't. Strong. Protective. Basically irresistible.

Pierce topped another hill, then stopped the truck and killed the engine. He pointed to the scene in front of them. "Get a load of this, and you'll see what I mean about the Double K getting into your blood."

Her breath caught as she scanned the area. They were parked beneath an aged oak tree. Two squirrels raced around its thick trunk. Three brilliantly colored blue jays jeered at them from their perches in the tangled, nearly bare branches.

Acres of rolling, fenced and cross-fenced pastures stretched off to the east. To the west was a rocky ledge that appeared to drop off dramatically. Beyond that was a creek that snaked its way into a heavily forested area.

Pierce climbed out of the truck and walked over to open her door. Before he could, she'd already jumped from the truck to a soft carpet of yellowing grass and dead oak leaves.

"I hear water," she said.

"Over here." He reached for her hand as he led her to the cliff's edge. "Watch your step and keep hold of my hand. Some of the smaller rocks can shift when you step on them."

They stopped at the edge of the gorge, her hand locked with a man she barely knew. Fear and uncertainty instead of exhilaration should have been swirling in her brain. How had she gotten to this place so quickly with Pierce after all she'd been through?

A gentle mist washed across her face. That was when she spotted the waterfall cascading down the slope of rocks to push its way into the creek below.

"It's truly breathtaking," she murmured.

"It's my favorite place on the ranch," Pierce admitted. "When attacks of grief at the loss of my parents made going forward almost impossible, I'd ride out here and somehow find an element of peace."

"It's hard to lose someone you love."

"You sound like you've been there."

"My grandfather," she said.

"Want to talk about it?"

She shook her head. She didn't want that terrifying brand of torment to shadow this special place.

Still holding tightly to her hand, Pierce led her to a huge rock that overlooked the waterfall. He leaned against the rough edges of the stone and then wrapped his arms around her waist from behind, pulling her against his chest.

The moment became pure magic. The beauty, the

protective sensation of his arms holding her tight, so close she could feel his warm breath on her neck.

For once, she let herself melt into the moment. No past. No future. Just the here and now, a second in time that she'd hold on to forever.

"Do you trust me, Grace?"

Chapter Ten

Did she trust Pierce Lawrence? It was a reasonable question. Crazily, she did trust him, but that didn't change anything.

She pulled away from him, desperate to keep a clear head. "I don't really know you well enough to give you a definitive answer, but I have no reason not to trust you at this point."

"Then level with me. Tell me what you're running from."

She'd feared this was coming but wasn't ready for it.

"I'm not running from anything."

"What about the boyfriend?"

She struggled to remember what she'd even said in that fabrication. "Things are fine. We both apologized and now we're moving on."

"You told Sheriff Cavazos today that you'd lost your job in Houston and that's why you're moving on."

"I didn't see any reason to share personal information with him when it had nothing to do with the shooting."

"If you're not running from anyone, why the disguise when you got here just two days ago?"

"I was experimenting with a new me and I'm sick and tired of bad relationships. I thought if I looked bad enough, no one would hit on me."

"You'd have to grow warts all over your face to keep that from happening."

"I'm not running away from anything," she insisted. "You're misreading me, Pierce. You don't really know me that well."

"I know your quick action likely saved my daughter's life today."

"I can't really take credit for that. It was all instinct."

"You don't have to be afraid of me, Grace. I'm not trying to take over your life and I'm definitely not trying to cause trouble for you. I just want to help. I can't do that unless you're honest with me."

"I am being honest with you."

She bit her bottom lip, hating the lies, actually aching to spill the whole truth to Pierce. He would hold her, assure her he could protect her from anything. He'd mean every word of it.

But no one won against Tom Lacoste and Grace could not pull Pierce into that. He had a precious daughter who needed him alive. And the horrifying truth was that even Jaci might not be safe if Tom thought killing Pierce's child would hurt Grace.

This was her fight. She'd made the mistakes that

had led to the nightmare. She'd made the choice that had led to her lonesome, loveless existence. She would pay the price.

Pierce caught her hand and pulled her back to face him. His gaze captured hers, intense, hypnotic.

"I'm here if you need me, Grace."

"How can you say that when you think I'm running away from something?"

"Because I don't believe you could ever do anything bad enough to deserve the fear you're living with."

"Why does any of this matter to you when it's doubtful we'll ever see each other again after this week?"

"It's the right thing to do. And I care. I like your warmth. I like the challenge of getting to know you. And I damn sure like the way you kiss."

Tears filled her eyes. Damn him. How could she have let him get that close? How could she let him tear down her resistance like that?

His lips met hers, gentle for a second and then ravaging. The passion swelled until it consumed Grace. Her hands slipped beneath Pierce's denim jacket and splayed across his back. She'd love to rip off that shirt and run her fingers across his bare back, trailing the sinewy muscles through the soft cotton of his shirt.

He pulled her ever tighter, lifted her and let her slide down the hard length of his need.

Heart pounding and gasping for breath, Grace finally managed to force herself back to sanity. She pushed away, but even that didn't cool the primal need that burned inside her.

"We should get back," she whispered.

"I hope you know what you're doing to me," he said, his voice husky with desire or perhaps frustration.

She didn't know what she was doing to him, but she was all too aware of what he was doing to her. That was wonderful and scary enough.

She walked back to the truck and he followed. Her emotions felt raw and exposed, as if he'd reached deep inside her and touched places that hadn't been touched before.

If his kiss affected her like that…what would making love with him do? Did she dare find out?

They talked very little on the short ride back to the house. When they drove up to the house, Jaci ran out the door and down the porch steps to meet them.

"We found the angels. And we found a manger and a baby Jesus. And guess what? Grandma has a dancing cowboy Santa that sings 'Frosty the Snowman.'"

"Did you two rob the Christmas store?"

"No. That's silly, Daddy. It was in Grandma's attic all the time. Can we go get the Christmas tree? Please."

"How about first thing in the morning? It's almost night and we can't find a good tree in the dark." Pierce reached down, picked up Jaci and swung her to his shoulders. "What is all this green stuff on the front porch?"

"It's garley. You have to hang it on the porch and put lights in it."

"Ah, garlands," Pierce said, "for decoration. But where did they come from?"

"We bought it on the way home. It smells like a Christmas tree."

"It smells wonderful," Grace agreed.

Mouthwatering odors from the kitchen, a three-foot-high maze of colorful plastic containers and a dancing Santa greeted them as they walked inside the house. Esther joined them from the kitchen, her limp barely noticeable. All the excitement no doubt over-shadowed the pain. Having Pierce and Jaci around was exactly what she'd needed.

But who wouldn't want them around?

"Don't tell me you got up in the attic on that bad ankle and hauled all of these boxes down," Pierce exclaimed.

"Land sakes, Pierce. You know I've got better sense than that. I had Buck do that. This is all the Christmas decorations I've collected over the past fifty-plus years."

"You think we need that many decorations?" he asked.

"We don't have to use them all. We've just got them handy in case we do. Right, Jaci?"

"Right," Jaci agreed. She stepped into an empty box and then jumped out.

Grace's knees literally grew weak.

A welcoming house. A happy family. Supper on the stove. Love and laughter.

Just as she'd envisioned the first time she'd seen

the house. Only in this case, reality topped her fantasy. And here she was right in the middle of it all. She didn't dare pinch herself, knowing it had to be a dream.

A very temporary dream.

PIERCE BUCKLED CHARLIE'S old leather tool belt around his waist and then rescued the aluminum extension ladder from behind a case of soft drinks and between a shovel and an old tin washtub.

The sun was diving toward the horizon, but he figured he had about forty-five minutes before it was full-fledged dark, just time enough to string the outdoor Christmas lights and garlands across the porch pillars and railings.

It would be one less thing he had to do tomorrow when he really wanted to start an assessment of the ranch's needs and assets. Besides, he needed a little physical exertion if he was going to keep eating Esther's Southern soul cooking.

Tonight it had been homemade beef and vegetable soup with corn bread. Vegetables from last summer's garden, the beef from the Double K Ranch. Healthy except that Pierce had slathered two hunks of corn bread in butter.

And he'd had to taste the cookies Jaci and Esther had baked this afternoon while he and Grace had been exploring the gorge at Lonesome Branch. More aptly, he'd been exploring his exploding attraction to the mysterious Grace Addison while she refused to be honest with him.

Here he was, doing it again, falling hard and at lightning speed for a woman he didn't understand. But this was far different than it had been when he fell for Leslie. Grace was different. He was different.

Back then, he'd just completed his SEAL training and was taking a walk on a San Diego beach when he literally ran into Leslie. He'd been cocky, confident and ready to party. She'd filled out a bikini to perfection, and when she'd asked him to rub sunscreen on her bare shoulders, he'd jumped at the invitation.

Two days later, they'd been married by a justice of the peace. Two weeks later, he'd left on assignment. Before he saw her again, he'd watched his best friend get blown up from an IED.

When Pierce came home, he was in another place. He tried to be the carefree young man Leslie had fallen in love with. He couldn't. The relationship never really got off the ground after that.

But then they had Jaci and that made it all worthwhile. He'd come home determined to be a good and loving father. All she had to do was wrap those little arms around him or say the word *daddy* and he was mush.

But he was still working on earning her trust. Hers and Grace's. Hopefully, strings of bright-colored lights and a little Christmas spirit would help with both of them.

Pierce scanned the garage for the claw hammer

and quickly spotted it hanging from Charlie's giant pegboard. Fact was everything in the old garage/ workshop was the way he remembered it. A full-blown vision of Charlie in his overalls, his guttural laugh spilling over the space, filled Pierce's mind.

A wave of nostalgia-flavored grief washed over him like a hard summer rain. Easy to understand why Charlie's death had about driven Esther crazy. There wasn't another man on the planet with a heart like Charlie's.

Suicide seemed impossible with a man like him. But murder? That possibility wouldn't quite jell, either.

Jaci ran into the garage as he attached the claw hammer to the tool belt. His little drama queen spun around like a dancer and then handed him a container. "Grandma Esther said you might need this."

He lifted the lid. Clips for hanging lights and greenery. "This is exactly what I needed."

"Can I help hang the lights?"

"Sure. You can be my supervisor."

"What's that?"

"The one who tells me how to do it."

"Okay." She went skipping out of the garage in front of him.

Jaci played with the garland while Pierce got started on the task at hand. He'd never hung Christmas lights before, but how difficult could it be?

He was halfway finished with the first pillar and feeling good about his success when he accidently knocked the carton of clips off the ladder's paint shelf.

"Sh… Ships, boats and canoes," he muttered, trying to cover his four-letter-word slip.

Jaci came running over. "What boat?"

"No boats. It's just something I say when I make a mess."

"I'll help you pick up the clips."

"That would be dandy."

"Dandy? You talk funny, Daddy."

"If you think that's funny, you should see me dance." He did a little two-step shuffle and then realized that Grace was at the door watching. He tipped his hat at her and went back to picking up the clips.

His phone vibrated. He slipped it from his back pocket and checked the caller ID. Leslie.

He'd tried to get in touch with her earlier without luck. He'd intended to tell her about the random shooting without Jaci around. He didn't want her to get Jaci upset, since his daughter was handling the frightening experience so well. Apparently, at age five, Christmas and ice cream took precedence over a mere shooting where no one got hurt.

He took the call before handing it off to Jaci—just in case she was calling with a problem.

"Hello. Christmas Central. How can I help you?"

"Is this Pierce?"

Divorced barely a week and she'd already forgotten his voice. Not that he cared at this point. "It's me. How are things in Cuba?"

"Interesting. How are things between you and Jaci?"

"Better than expected. We're having quite the adventure." He wouldn't mention the shooting in front of Jaci.

"Are you in Texas?" Leslie asked.

"We are. Got some bad news when we arrived."

"What was that?"

"Charlie died a few months back, but we're going to stay on here at the ranch and have Christmas with Esther."

"Do try to make it feel like Christmas for Jaci, Pierce. It's important. We've always had a tree, not a real one, of course. They're so messy when those nasty needles get stuck in the carpet."

"Needles are funny that way."

"Must you make a joke of everything? Put Jaci on the phone, please."

"Okay, hold on a second."

"One more thing."

"I'm washing behind her ears just like you said."

"Keep her off the horses. They're too dangerous."

"I'm not letting her do anything dangerous. Here's Jaci." He handed the phone to his daughter. "It's your mom."

Jaci was so excited she jumped up and down, and then she began talking so fast that he doubted Leslie could understand half of what she was saying.

Pierce went back to hanging the lights and garlands but had no trouble hearing Jaci's end of the conversation. Talk of ice cream cones, baking cookies, dancing Santas and silver slippers for the Christmas tree. The only mention of anything vaguely connected to the shooting was that she had a boo-boo on her elbow and that Esther had put a bandage on it.

Nothing in the chatter Leslie could fault him for until Jaci started talking about her ride on Dreamer. Oh, well. Leslie was in Cuba and he and Jaci were in Texas on an adventure.

There were three things any Texas adventure should include: a Stetson, a pair of genuine cowboy boots and a horse. As his SEAL buddy from New Orleans used to say, everything else was lagniappe.

Grace was lagniappe-plus and probably trouble with a capital *T*. And he was falling for her much too hard and too fast.

"GREAT JOB," GRACE said as she stepped back into the house after checking out Pierce's handiwork. She walked over and backed up to the roaring fireplace to warm her backside.

"Your nose is red," Esther said. "Is it that cold out there, already?"

"Cold enough that it didn't take me long to look at the lights."

"They're predicting a chance of frost by morning," Esther said. "You might want to put off finding that perfect Christmas tree for a day or two."

"No. Not put it off," Jaci protested, looking up from a Christmas storybook—another attic find. "We can wear coats. You promised, Daddy."

"A cowboy can't break a promise. If it's a tree you

want, we're getting a tree. We'll just have to bundle up like it's a snow day."

Another thing to add to the growing list of things Grace admired about Pierce. He kept his word to Jaci.

Grace left the fireplace and settled in the empty recliner. Jaci closed her book and crawled into Grace's lap. "Let's go outside and see how pretty the house looks with all the lights on it."

"I just did that," Grace reminded her. "You and your dad did a fantastic job with the decorating."

"He did the work. I just played."

"You kept him company," Esther said. "That's important, too."

"Couldn't have done it without you," Pierce agreed.

"If everyone's going out to get the tree in the morning, I guess I'll just have to put on my big red parka and rough it with you," Esther said. "I'll make us a big thermos of hot chocolate to keep our insides warm."

"Sounds like a winner to me," Pierce said. "I think the coldest I've ever been was that night Charlie took my entire football team on a hayride up to Lonesome Branch."

"I remember that night," Esther said. "I tried to talk him into postponing that for a warmer night, too. I mean, it's not like we get that many frigid nights this far south. He wouldn't hear of it. You guys were celebrating a divisional win if I remember that right."

"Right. And then we were slaughtered at the following game. But that didn't take anything away from our celebration. We huddled under blankets for the ride and then got out and roasted hot dogs and marshmallows around a bonfire with our teeth chattering."

"I can't believe it was that much fun if it was freezing," Grace said. "It must have been your first hayride."

"First hayride we got to take dates."

"Now the plot thickens."

"What's roasted marshmallows?" Jaci asked.

"You stick a marshmallow on a stick with a point on it and then poke it over a fire."

"And burn it?"

"You don't have to, but the burned ones taste the best."

"I have marshmallows, chocolate candy bars and Graham crackers," Esther said. "Anyone up for s'mores?"

"Count me in," Grace said. "Haven't had one of those since my Girl Scouts days."

"Okay, guys. That's enough begging." Pierce stood and put his hands out as if he were surrendering. "Let me grab my coat and I'll have a campfire going outside in ten minutes."

Jaci hopped across the room. "Goody. Goody. We're gonna burn up marshmallows."

"I'll make some hot chocolate," Grace offered.

True to his word, Pierce had the fire blazing by the time they made it to the campfire he'd started in the backyard. They couldn't see the Christmas lights from there, but heaven was putting on a show of its own. It was like someone had thrown a million diamonds into the air and they'd stuck on a mat of black velvet.

"Texas stars," Pierce said when he saw her admiring them. "Not like this anywhere else."

"I'm pretty sure Texas doesn't have its own Milky Way," Grace said.

"You'll change your mind about that, after you've been deep in the heart of the Lone Star State for a while."

But she wouldn't be there awhile. She needed to leave at sunup, before she lost her heart so completely to this whole wonderful family that she'd never be able to say goodbye.

They'd finished off the s'mores and were sitting around the fire in folding outdoor chairs and sipping hot chocolate when Pierce's phone rang.

He checked the ID. "Sheriff Cavazos. I better take this."

Jaci walked over and climbed into Grace's lap. Grace tried to fight back her anxiety over why the sheriff was calling back tonight.

She kissed the top of Jaci's head and cuddled her close. "I think someone's getting sleepy."

"Will you give me a bath and read me a story?"

"Of course."

The perfect night was about to come to an abrupt end. Grace was looking at Pierce and even in the firelight she could tell that the news he was getting from the sheriff was not good.

"THE WOMAN YOU were with today is not who she claims to be. I just thought you and Esther would like to know."

Chapter Eleven

Pierce had known from the beginning that Grace carried secrets and fears that wouldn't let her be herself. He wasn't that surprised that the social security number she'd given Sheriff Cavazos was fake. The number belonged to a woman from Buffalo, New York, who had died over ten years ago.

There were plenty of places to get fake IDs, driver's licenses, social security cards, even passports if you had the money to pay for one. The worry was why she needed one.

He couldn't make himself believe that she'd committed a crime so terrible that she'd had to go on the run and lose herself in a new identity. He'd seen evil in men's eyes more than once. He saw only goodness in Grace's.

Or had he fallen so hard for her that he couldn't see past his testosterone? Was it possible he was putting his daughter and even Esther in danger because he was falling in love with Grace?

He stared into the dying embers of the campfire,

the cold having crawled so deep inside him he didn't feel it any longer. The others had all gone inside at least an hour ago.

Jaci had wanted Grace—not him—to help her bathe and to tuck her into bed. Like Esther, she'd bonded almost instantly with Grace. Could they all be wrong about her?

As the final sparks turned to ash, he grabbed the hose and sprayed down the campfire until there was no danger of the wind stirring the flames again.

There was a light on in the kitchen, but he fully expected everyone to be in bed when he stepped inside the back door. Instead, Esther was sitting at the table munching on a cookie.

"Did you finally decide to come in?"

"I had a lot on my mind."

"I noticed. What did the sheriff have to say that threw you into such a dark place?"

"Was it that evident?"

"It was to me. I'm sure it was to Grace, too."

His first urge was to tell Esther the truth, but he had to talk to Grace about this first. He owed her that much. But he did have questions for Esther.

"I heard today that Charlie's friend Dudley Miles is in prison."

"He is. At least Charlie wasn't alive to see it. He thought so highly of Dudley. It would have killed him to see his friend up on the stand admitting what he'd done to that poor little boy."

Pierce pulled out a kitchen chair and straddled it. "Exactly what did Dudley do?"

"He was home alone with his four-year-old grandson, Kyle. He had a few drinks and fell asleep, or passed out as the prosecutor said. Apparently, the boy climbed up on the kitchen counter and then fell off and landed on his head. He was dead when Dudley found him."

"Poor guy. And poor kid. Was that Angela's son?"

"Yeah. Do you remember her?"

"She was a couple of years behind me in school, but I remember she was a spoiled brat and a real pain. In fact, that kind of irresponsibility sounds a lot more like her than Dudley."

"That's exactly what Charlie said before he was murdered. He was convinced Dudley was totally innocent."

"Then this all happened just a few months ago?"

"Yes. Dudley confessed it all less than two weeks after Charlie's death. Confessed to not watching the boy properly and more."

"More?"

"He took the lifeless body of his grandson and buried it in the woods. It wasn't found for almost a month, time Angela believed the boy had been kidnapped. You can imagine how frantic she and her mother were. And all the while Dudley was pretending he was looking for the missing boy."

"That doesn't even make sense. It was an accident. Why would he get rid of the body?"

"They went over and over that during the trial. The prosecutor claimed Dudley was afraid of facing his family and of facing charges after his failure to watch the boy had led to his death. But then Dudley admitted to everything. I have to think he just temporarily lost his mind when he found his grandson dead."

"Still doesn't make sense unless that's not how the boy really died."

Esther dabbed at her eyes with a napkin. "Sometimes I think it's even worse for Millie than it is for me. She lost her grandson to death and her husband to prison. But at least she still has a daughter. I have no one."

Pierce reached across the table and laid a hand on top of hers. "You're not alone, Esther. I may not always be here in the house, but I promise I will be in your life from now on."

"I appreciate that, but you boys have your own lives. It's none of my business, but if you let Grace Addison get away from you, I think you're making a huge mistake."

"That may not be my choice."

"It is. I can see the way she looks at you and the way you look at her. From my viewpoint it's pretty obvious that you two are crazy about each other. A woman can always see those things."

Even if she was right, that didn't guarantee him a choice. He walked Esther back to her bedroom. Knowing he still wouldn't be able to sleep, he tiptoed down the hall and stopped at the closed door to where Grace was sleeping.

He'd like nothing more than to go in, wake her up and beg her to finally tell him the truth.

No. He'd like nothing better than to crawl into bed with her and hold her body next to his. He ached to make love with her.

No matter what she'd done, he wanted her so badly he could feel it in every cell in his body.

Instead, he turned and walked away. If they were to have a chance, it was up to her. She had to trust him enough to admit the truth.

THE ROOM WAS DARK but not empty. She could hear breathing and the sound of footsteps coming closer. Bloodred eyes stared at her as a hand closed around her throat.

"Did you really think you could get by with destroying me, Grace? Did you think I wouldn't make you pay?"

Fear paralyzed her. This couldn't be happening. Tom was in prison. She was trapped in a nightmare. She tried to scream, but his hands on her neck choked and silenced the attempt.

A low maniacal laughter echoed through her brain. He moved his face closer to hers. The smell of alcohol overpowered her senses, made her dizzy as if she was the one who was drunk.

The fingers of his free hand trailed her cleavage

and then pinched her right nipple so hard she winced in pain.

"I've missed you so much my beautiful nympho. You do remember the fun we had together, don't you, sweetheart? At first when you were so crazy about me you couldn't keep your hands off me." He straddled her, holding her down with his body.

He was going to force himself on her again, painfully, humiliatingly, the way he had so many nights after he tired of torturing her. Her stomach retched. She didn't care. She'd love to throw up in his taunting face.

He removed his hand from her throat. It still hurt to breathe, but air pushed into her lungs. He held her hands over her head, shoving them hard into the bed.

She could see him clearly now, but he didn't look like the Tom she remembered. His eyes and his unearthly grin made him look like a demon.

"Sex was so much more satisfying after you turned against me, the games we played much more creative after you decided you were too good for me."

"I was too good for you. I am too good for you. You are a vile, repulsive murderer. You kill people in cold blood."

"Only those who deserve it, the ones who double-cross me the way you did."

"You killed my grandfather. He was a helpless old man in a wheelchair and you shot him dead in his own home like a rabid dog. He never did anything to you. He never did anything mean to anyone."

"You have only yourself to blame for his death, lovely Grace. I live by a code. A simple rule that serves me well. Double-cross me and you and anyone you love pays. But let's not waste time talking about the past. We have so many new things to discuss."

His grip loosened on her right hand just long enough for her to break free. She clawed at his face, her nails digging into his flesh. He slapped her hard across the face.

Somehow she managed to clasp her hand around the base of the bedside lamp. Tom wrenched it from her hand and hurled it across the room.

He leaned over and put his mouth to her ear. "Don't worry, sweetheart. I won't kill you yet. I have surprises to show you first."

He yanked her from the bed. She fell to the floor and he crushed her chest with his foot and then picked her up by the hair.

"You cut your hair. I told you to never cut your hair. You did it for him, didn't you?"

"I don't know who you're talking about."

"Of course you do. I'm talking about your lover. You think he's going to save you. Big, tough cowboy. He died begging me to let him live, just as your grandfather did. Just as you will when the time is right."

No. No. No. This was a nightmare. If she fought it hard enough, she would wake up and she would be in her own bed in Tennessee.

No. Not in Tennessee. She was in Texas.

She tried to run. Her legs refused to move. Wake up. She had to wake up.

She couldn't. This was too real. Tom was dragging her across the room and she had no strength to fight him off.

"Tell me what you miss most about me, Grace. The hot wax dripping onto your nipples? Or is it the bodies that littered our beautiful home in the wee hours of the morning?"

"That was a long time ago. Please go away. Let me have a life. Please. Just let me have a life."

"That's right. Beg. I love it when you whine and beg. You can have your life. You're already dead to me. But first, the surprise."

She grabbed hold of the bedpost and held on until he tore her fingers from the wood and almost from her hands. She closed her eyes and prayed for the nightmare to end.

Tom opened a door. "Here's your life, Grace. Open your eyes and see all the gifts I brought you."

She opened her eyes, afraid to look, more afraid not to. Three bodies lay on the floor, facedown, with nothing to cover them but shredded sheets.

Tom kicked the first one, rolling it over. Grace stared into the dead eyes. No. No. It couldn't be. "She was only a little girl."

"You knew the code. You broke the rules."

Her heart beat so hard she could feel it clawing its way out of her chest.

Finally, screams tore from her throat.

"Kill me, Tom. Kill me, you rotten son of a bitch, and then kill yourself. The devil is tired of waiting on your soul."

His laugh was the last thing she heard before she felt her heart explode.

Chapter Twelve

The agonizing screams punctured Pierce's sleep. His eyes flew open and he jerked to a sitting position. His mind spun, trying to focus on the urgency that ripped through him. Screams? Or had sleep pulled him back into battle?

The screams started again, piercing, chilling, as if someone's heart had been ripped out and tossed to a pack of wild hogs.

Not Jaci. She was in the room next to him.

Grace!

He jumped out of bed naked, grabbed his jeans and yanked them on, though he didn't waste time zipping them. He heard Esther's footsteps close behind him as he raced down the hallway.

"I've got it," he called without slowing down or looking back. "You check on Jaci. I don't want her alone and frightened if the screams wake her." He barged through Grace's door. Panic cracked him across the ribs like a two-by-four when he saw her bed.

The quilt was on the floor. Crimson-smeared

sheets were pulled down so far he could see the right corner of the mattress. Sharp-edged chunks of ceramic from a busted lamp were scattered like river rocks over a dry creek bed.

Finally, he spotted Grace. She was curled up fetal-style on the floor in the far corner of the room. Eyes closed. Not moving. His heart thundered in his chest as he rushed across the room and kneeled to check her pulse.

It was beating strong. The rush of relief made it difficult to breathe. He touched a hand to her forehead. She opened her eyes and tears spilled from the corners and ran down her cheeks.

"What happened in here?" he asked.

Grace pulled herself to a sitting position but leaned against the wall for support. "I had a nightmare."

"Must have been a humdinger."

Grace nodded but didn't elaborate. No doubt she was still in shock. So was he. This looked like a scene from a horror movie just after the psycho paid a visit.

Pierce left her alone long enough to slip into her bathroom and wet a cloth. When he got back to her, she was looking more alert and staring at the bloodied scratches on her hands and forearms.

"I've never scratched myself until bleeding in a nightmare before," she said.

"Probably happened when you cracked the lamp over someone's head."

"I don't remember doing that."

He zipped his jeans and then went back to Grace.

He wiped her face with the cool cloth and then washed the already dried blood from her hands. "Do you remember the rest of the nightmare?" he asked.

"The worst of it." She tried to stand, but she swayed and almost fell. Pierce caught her before she did. This had been no ordinary nightmare and the hell of it clearly still had a hold on her.

He lifted her into his arms and carried her to the rocking chair near the window. Her cotton gown was damp, her skin clammy.

He took her on his lap, cuddled her close and rocked her like a baby. Pierce knew next to nothing about psychology, but he'd seen firsthand on the battlefield what living with constant fear and danger could do to a person.

He was more certain than ever that Grace was running scared. That fear had erupted tonight in her subconscious. But she couldn't go on like this. He had to find a way to make her see that.

"I'm here, Grace," he said softly in a tone he hoped was reassuring. "The nightmare was just that. It can't hurt you. I won't let anything hurt you. Not tonight. Not ever."

The moment the words left his mouth, he knew they were more than empty promises. When he'd heard her screams and then walked into the room to find her in that petrified state, his heart passed the point of no return.

He wasn't just in heat, he loved her. It might make no sense, but it was true all the same. He'd do anything to help her escape whatever she was running from, but he couldn't do it unless she let him.

"Do you want to talk about the nightmare?"

"It wouldn't help."

She was closing him out again, but this time he wouldn't let her. Her life might be at stake.

"Have you had this same nightmare before?"

"Far too often." She looked around. "But I've never destroyed a room like this before."

"Maybe the nightmare is trying to tell you something."

"Oh, it told me something, okay. It made its message nauseatingly clear." She pulled herself out of his arms and walked over to lean against the foot of the bed.

"It's time I move on and leave you, Jaci and Esther to celebrate your terrific family Christmas without me and my problems."

"We're not the scary ones, Grace. We're not giving you the nightmares. I don't know what's happened in your past, but I do know if you don't deal with it, the nightmares are never going to end."

"You don't know what I'm facing, Pierce. You're strong and brave and decent and I know you want to help me now. But if you knew the truth, you'd be packing my bags for me this minute."

He walked over and took both her hands in his. "Try me."

"Please, just let this go, Pierce."

"You know I can't do that."

"Because you're a former navy SEAL?"

"Because I care about you. I care about you a lot, and judging from your kisses, I think you like me, too."

"I care about you, Jaci and Esther, which is why I can't drag any of you into my private terror."

"You aren't dragging me. I'm begging to be included."

"You'll be sorry."

"Fine. Tell me what's really got you scared half to death, and if I want out, I'll let you know."

"You're not going to give up, are you?"

"Nope."

"Okay. You've asked for it, but first I need a shower."

"I'll wash your back."

"We'll save that until you know what you're getting into."

He could live with that. He ached to kiss her, but somehow the timing didn't seem right. This was about a lot more than a moment of passion. He had a feeling his whole life was about to change.

He just wasn't sure in what direction it was heading.

GRACE WAS AN emotional train wreck when she stepped out of the shower. The images from the nightmare refused to go away.

All dead. All dead. All dead. A mantra straight

from her hellish past, a thread that had echoed through her mind and soul for the past six years.

But then there was Pierce Lawrence, a man who represented everything her heart longed for. She'd promised him the truth and he'd get it. She owed him that much.

She buffed her body and then her hair with a fluffy white towel. Her body trembled as she pulled on the clean cotton nightshirt she'd brought into the bathroom with her and then slipped into a pair of matching pink panties.

Neither was particularly sexy, though she was keenly aware of the sensual temptation every time she was near Pierce. But tonight even that was overshadowed by the terror of her past.

She applied some of the ointment the doctor had given her to the scratches on her hands and arms and checked the bandage on her temple. Satisfied she hadn't ripped out her stitches, she worked a comb through the tangles in her damp hair.

She joined Pierce in the bedroom to find that he'd remade the bed and turned down the covers—on both sides of the bed. The pillows on both sides were also piled against the headboard.

She'd assumed he would sit in the chair while they talked. Sitting in bed, side by side, would make this even more difficult for her. But once Pierce knew the truth, the sizzling attraction between them would go ice-cold.

He'd be over her. She'd be gone.

"There's still time to run for the hills," she said.

"Not a chance, but I was beginning to think you'd slipped out the bathroom window and did that yourself."

"It crossed my mind."

"I would only hunt you down."

"I figured that. Thanks for straightening the mess."

"It wasn't that difficult. I took the busted lamp and its parts to the kitchen trash and found clean sheets on the top shelf of the bedroom closet."

"You make a neat bed."

"Military-style. We don't mess around."

She walked over and crawled into bed, pushed her back and head against the pillows and pulled the covers up to her knees. Pierce slid in beside her.

There was nowhere to start except with the mistake that had thrown her life into disaster mode.

"My name is Grace, but the last name is not Addison. It's Lacoste. I was married for a time to the infamous Tom Lacoste."

"The name sounds familiar."

"Wilbert Lacoste was Tom's father. He was the head honcho of the New Orleans drug dealing operations during the last decade."

"Now that you mention it, I do remember something about that. Was that the notorious drug-running family taken down by a college coed?"

"Right."

"Wait. That was you. You were that coed. That's why you're on the run."

"I wasn't actually attending college when I testi-fied, but I was when I met and married Tom Lacoste."

He reached for her hand, but she pulled it away. "There's a lot more to the story. If you give me the least bit of sympathy, I may never get through this."

And for some reason, now that she'd admitted that much out loud for the first time since the trial, she needed to say these disgusting truths out loud.

Pierce put his hands behind his head. "I'll do my best."

"Deal. I'll start at the beginning. Perhaps you can get a better grip on this than I ever have."

Though it was difficult, she tried to let her mind drift back to a time before she'd invited a charismatic, wealthy, powerful cold-blooded killer into her life.

"I grew up in the little town of Decatur, Missis-sippi. I don't remember my parents. My mother died of a drug overdose when I was two. There was no father's name on my birth certificate. I was raised by my grandparents, two of the most loving, giving people on the face of the earth. A lot like Esther."

"Are they still alive?"

Grace squeezed her eyes shut to fight back gath-ering tears and then blinked them repeatedly as the past pulled her into its depths.

"My grandmother died of cancer my senior year in high school, right after my academic success earned me a full scholarship to Tulane University in New Orleans."

"So you were a brainiac."

"A very naive one who had no experience with big-city life. I was still grieving for my grandmother when I left for college. Within two weeks of reaching the Big Easy, I was introduced to the very active music and bar scene in and around the university area."

"And no doubt that's where you ran into Tom Lacoste."

"I did. Only, he was the rescuer that night. He claimed he saw one of the male students I was with slip a powder into my drink. He had the guy thrown out and then moved in on me himself.

"I was so naive I not only bought the lie about the powder but quickly fell in love with this sophisticated and charming older guy."

"How much older?"

"I was eighteen. He was thirty-two. I suppose in his own way he fell in love with me, too. We were married less than a month later in a chapel in Las Vegas."

"And you had no idea what he was involved in?"

"No. A possibility like that never crossed my mind. I knew the family was incredibly wealthy and thought it a bit strange that they never talked about their work. I would have never married a cold-blooded killer, had I had even an inkling of the truth."

"When did you find out what he was really like?"

"About a month after we returned from our honeymoon in Italy. By then I was more in love with him than ever. I wanted to bring my grandfather down to meet him, but he kept putting me off. So I went to see my grandfather to break the news to him that I was married and dropping out of Tulane."

"How did that go?"

"Not well. I could tell he was really worried about me, but I thought he was just upset that I was dropping out of school. I left Mississippi two days earlier than planned to get back to my new life and Tom. That was the last time I ever saw my grandfather alive."

Pierce pulled her trembling body into his arms. This time she didn't pull away.

"You don't have to say more tonight. We can finish this discussion in the morning after you've had some rest and time to regroup from the nightmare."

"No. I have to get through this now."

She told him about the doorbell ringing in the middle of the night. Tom had ordered her to stay in the bedroom until he returned no matter what she heard. She had stayed through the loud, angry voices and the sound of more people arriving.

And then she'd heard gunshots. Rapid-fire like it had been today. She screamed and went running to the back of the house where the men had gathered.

Blood pooled on Tom's office floor. Two men lay dead, their brains spilling out of their skulls. Tom ordered her to stay out of it. She cowered in the corner and watched while he raised his gun and put a bullet through his best friend's head, too.

The words spilled from her mouth now. How she'd

threatened to go to the police. How she'd been locked in an upstairs bedroom for weeks, raped and tortured in ways it still made her sick to talk about. In an instant she'd gone from wife to imprisoned sex slave.

"As bad as that was, the worst was the day Tom walked in and tossed a photograph onto my bed. It was my grandfather's body, slumped over in his wheelchair, a bullet through the front of his head."

Pierce sputtered a string of curses. "Sorry. I couldn't hold that in any longer. If I ever get my hands on Tom Lacoste, I'll kill him. I swear, I'll kill him. But surely the Lacostes are still in prison."

"Yes, and hopefully he'll remain there until the day he dies. But that doesn't mean he doesn't have goons on the outside still eager to do his bidding."

Pierce eased his arm from around her, stood and started pacing the room. "So you've been living in fear for what? Six years? Seven?"

"Almost six. I was in protective custody throughout the trial and for the first two years after Tom was convicted. Other members of the Lacoste family were still being prosecuted at the time. I've been on the run on my own since then.

"Relying on fake IDs. Staying as low-key as possible. Avoiding personal relationships. Changing my appearance as much as possible. I even considered cosmetic surgery to change my nose and chin, but I couldn't afford it."

"What made you leave where you were before driving to Texas?"

"Mostly intuition," she admitted. "I was working in a library in a small mountain town in Tennessee. I ran into a stranger a couple of times and something about the way he stared at me made me nervous. The final straw was when he came into the library where I worked and I caught him taking my picture with his phone."

"I can't believe every man you've ever met doesn't follow you around and want your picture, but under the circumstances I can see why you became suspicious. The shooting in Winding Creek must have terrified you."

"It didn't help any. But that's why I can't stay here and share your wonderful Christmas. My being here puts you all in danger. The Lacostes don't just murder in cold blood the people they think double-crossed them. They kill their enemies' friends and family members, the same way they killed my grandfather. My staying here puts you all at risk."

Pierce spun around and stared at her as if she'd grown a second head. "Your leaving is all about protecting us?"

"Yes. It makes sense."

"It's insane. You can't keep running from this lunatic your whole life. You've paid your dues. You deserve a life, a real life where you can stop punishing yourself for doing the right thing."

This was what she'd been afraid of all along. Instead of kicking her out, he wanted to save her.

Pierce walked back to the bed and sat down on the edge on her side.

"Listen up, sweetheart. You're not going anywhere, at least not out of fear of some has-been incarcerated criminal. I can assure you I've taken on tougher than him."

"But there's not just you to consider, Pierce. There's Esther and Jaci."

"I'm considering them. That doesn't mean I'm throwing you to the wolves. Families stick together."

"I'm not family."

"Give me time. I'm working on that. It's late and you need your rest. We'll talk more about this in the morning, but don't try anything stupid like going on the run again. If you do, I'll be the one tracking you down."

"What sense does it make for me to stay here?"

"'Cause we're going to have the mostest best Christmas ever," Pierce said, playfully mocking Jaci, even though he sounded dead serious. "And because I owe you a horseback riding lesson."

He leaned over and kissed her, sweeter and more gentle than before. Then he walked over and lay down next to her.

"Don't worry. I'm not planning to seduce you, Grace. When we make love for the first time, I want it to be so special we remember it for the rest of our lives.

"Tonight I'm just going to lie here until you fall

into a peaceful sleep. It's time for those nightmares of yours to ride off the edge of a cliff."

"You're an amazing man, Pierce Lawrence."

"You ain't seen nothing yet."

PIERCE WOKE AT sunrise to a pleasurable throbbing in his groin. It took only a second to realize the reason for that. The soft weight resting on his thigh was Grace's leg. The silky brown hair haloed across his left shoulder belonged to her, as well.

He'd known it would be risky when he'd shed his jeans in the middle of the night. But the scratchy denim, while it didn't come close to the more serious problems robbing him from sleep, was the only distraction he could safely do anything about.

The marvel was he'd fallen asleep at all lying this close to Grace. His unwanted erection swelled. If he didn't get up now, his body was likely to override his brain.

He'd meant what he said last night. The first time they made love with each other should be memorable—for all the right reasons. Not as an act of frustration on the heels of a devastating nightmare.

Struggling to control his libido, Pierce eased away from Grace as gently as he could, stopping and holding his breath for a second when she stirred. Her eyes never opened and her breathing fell right back into a rhythmic pattern of sleep. After last night, she had every reason to be exhausted.

Her bizarre and frightening revelations came back

to him in gory detail as he wiggled back into his jeans. The thought of her being sexually abused and tortured by that monster of a husband filled Pierce with rage.

Prison was too good for the pyscho. A slow, painful death was too good as well, but at least that would make Grace feel a hell of a lot safer. And if Pierce was the one doing the killing, he would definitely feel justified.

It wouldn't be the first time he'd ever killed a human being. He'd done it before in battle to save lives, but it was something a man never fully got over. His SEAL teammates felt the same.

So how could a man like Tom Lacoste kill and torture so casually? Was it a gene defect? Greed? An experience in his youth? Or did some people have a malfunction in their brain that spewed hate and evil?

Pierce stopped at the door and looked back at Grace. She was naturally beautiful inside and out. Proof of that was in the way she'd bonded with Esther and Jaci.

Pierce wasn't exactly sure how he'd handle this yet, but he knew he'd give his life to keep her safe if it came to that. He hoped it wouldn't. He planned to spend the rest of his days enjoying his life with her. And his nights? Well, those would be heaven.

All he had to do was convince her of that.

He crept through the house hoping not to wake anyone else. He made a pot of coffee, took a mug to his room with him and turned on his computer. A few seconds later Google had responded to his command and supplied him with countless references to Tom Lacoste.

He zeroed in on the first one and double clicked. The headline punched him below the belt. His wish to face Tom Lacoste head-on might be granted.

Chapter Thirteen

Tom Lacoste, part of the murderous Lacoste family who ruled the New Orleans illegal drug market for years, is being released from prison. Convicted on seven different counts of murder in the first degree and of imprisoning and torturing his teenage wife, Lacoste was informed that his life sentence was cut short today.

His release was ordered after Judge Wallerton determined that evidence used in his trial was obtained without proper warrants.

"Son of a bitch."

Pierce slammed a fist against the desk. What a bunch of garbage. He muttered a few curses that he couldn't hold back.

How could that have happened? Grace's testimony alone should have been enough to keep the man in prison until he was gasping for his last breath.

Pierce checked the date of the article. It had been written eight days ago. That meant Tom Lacoste had been walking the streets a free man for over a week. Grace would freak out when she heard this.

He'd love to keep it from her until he had the chance to check out a few details, like where Tom Lacoste was now and if there was any surveillance in place.

Keeping anything from Grace at this point would be a bad decision. She'd finally trusted him enough to spill her guts to him. He didn't want to lose that trust.

He'd tell her right after they got back from the hunt for a perfect Christmas tree. No use to spoil that for her. She'd been robbed of enough Christmases already.

Grace's first impulse on finding her ex was walking the streets a free man would be to run. A few minor mechanical adjustments to her car's engine could make sure that didn't happen. In fact, Pierce would take care of that right now.

The easy way is always mined.

One of Murphy's laws of combat. Why in hell was that popping into his mind right now?

Jaci jumped from the backseat of Pierce's truck and threw up her hands. "This must be the North Pole?"

"I'm pretty sure we're still in Texas," Grace said, correcting her but loving her exuberance.

"Then how come there's so many Christmas trees here?"

"They're not actually Christmas trees," Pierce said. "They're evergreens, which just happen to make beautiful Christmas trees. But you're right. It does seem like these trees should be near Santa's workshop."

"Except there's no snow," Jaci said. "The North Pole always has snow."

"Don't get a lot of snow in these parts," Pierce said.

"We do get a few flakes every now and then," Esther said. "I remember one Christmas Charlie and I woke up to what looked like a winter wonderland.

"We saddled up my horse Elvis and Charlie's black steed and we went riding through the snow up to the falls at the gorge. What a ride that was."

"If it snows this Christmas, I could ride Dreamer," Jaci said.

"Don't go counting on snow for Christmas," Pierce cautioned. "Even Santa can't promise that. But you can still ride Dreamer."

"Can I get Dreamer a Christmas present?"

"That's a great idea," Esther said. "A big, red juicy apple would make a nice gift for Dreamer. She loves apples."

"I can give her an apple and a carrot," Jaci said. "But not a candy cane. She might get sick."

"Actually, Dreamer is fond of peppermints," Esther said. "But it's probably not a good idea to give her too many treats at once."

"Mommy says too much candy will give me a stomachache."

"And that's a fact," Pierce said.

Grace was impressed with the way Pierce handled

the situation when Jaci talked about her mother. If he felt any animosity toward his ex-wife, he didn't show it in front of his daughter.

"Look," Jaci called. "I found us a tree." She ran to a nearby tree and hugged it, a pine that was much too tall and wide to fit in Esther's living room.

"That one's nice," Pierce said, "but we can't take the first one you see. We gotta take our time and find the perfect tree to hang those silver slippers on."

He picked up Jaci, swung her to his shoulders and off they went, trekking up a hilltop where young pines, cedars and an occasional juniper dotted the landscape.

"You were right," Grace said to Esther. "There are plenty to choose from. Shall we tag along?"

"You go ahead," Esther said. "This cold weather has my arthritis acting up. Between that and the soreness in my ankle, I think I'm better off just sitting in the nice warm truck."

"You're sure you don't mind being left alone?"

"Honey, every foot of this ranch is home to me. I'll be just fine. You go catch up with them. Pierce and Jaci will be disappointed if you don't help pick out that tree."

Grace hurried off in the direction where they'd disappeared into the trees. She had no trouble following the sound of Jaci's excited voice and laughter.

Jaci was ecstatic about Christmas in the way only kids could be. Grace knew how happy Pierce was that she was adjusting to her mother's absence and making great strides in warming up to him.

Nonetheless, Grace could tell his good mood this morning was forced. Not that she'd expect anything different after the horror tales she'd laid on him last night.

She'd shared things with Pierce that she'd never shared with another living soul. Some of the torture she told him about had been so humiliating and degrading she hadn't even described them to her lawyers.

She would understand completely if he'd changed his mind and was having second thoughts about wanting her around. What man wouldn't?

Grace hadn't seen or heard him climb out of her bed this morning, but he'd been gone when she woke up. Being that eager to escape a woman's bedroom said a lot.

Yet he'd been insistent she come with them this morning.

"There you are," he said when she caught up with them. "I was starting to think you'd bailed on us in favor of the warm truck."

"And miss picking out the world's best ever Christmas tree? You think I'm crazy or something?"

"Actually, I think you're pretty fine." He smiled and reached out a hand to her. Warmth flushed her body and a traitorous frisson rocked her senses. A smile. A touch. That was all it took from him to brighten the colors of her world.

She was falling hard, but was he? Or had last night's confessions changed everything for him?

They walked on in the quiet hush of a cold winter morning in the breathtakingly beautiful Texas Hill Country. At least quiet until Jaci's high-pitched voice shattered the silence.

"Look, Daddy. Reindeer." She pointed toward a buck and three does standing not ten feet away from them. The does took off running at the sound of her voice.

The buck stood stone still, looking straight at them with incredibly captivating brown eyes. Finally, he raised his head higher and turned away, quickly disappearing into the trees.

"That's the tree I want, Daddy. The tree the reindeer like. It's perfect for the silver slippers."

"I agree," Grace said, thankful this choice was a really good one. The tree was a pine with an abundance of full branches to hold the lights and ornaments, around seven feet tall, with bright green needles and a shape to rival the artificial tree they'd seen in town.

"Who can argue with reindeer?" Pierce said. "Although those aren't actually reindeer."

"How do you know?"

"Reindeer look a little different and there aren't any around these parts."

"They look like deer."

"They are deer—white-tailed deer. But I bet these

are the kind of deer Santa would use to pull his sleigh if he lived in Texas."

"Can they fly?"

"Nope." Pierce laughed, no doubt realizing his logic was not meshing with Jaci's fanciful reality. "Guess Santa better stick to Rudolph and the rest of his reindeer team."

Pierce swung Jaci back to the ground. "You two stay right here and make sure we don't lose this tree and I'll go back to the truck to grab my ax."

"We're cutting down a Christmas tree. We're cutting down a Christmas tree." Jaci made a song of the words, clapping along and dancing to her own joyful music.

Grace had music, too, but it was playing in her mind and in her heart, a song her grandmother used to sing about being home for Christmas. Grace had given up on ever having a real home again, much less spending Christmas in one.

She'd given up on Christmas trees and silver ornaments and bright-colored lights. Given up on joy. Given up on Christmas.

But she couldn't deny that she wanted this Christmas at the Double K Ranch, wanted it so desperately she could feel it glowing inside her. It might have to last her a lifetime.

Pierce returned a few minutes later, a large ax in hand.

"Stand back. This is a very dangerous tool."

He held the ax back and then swung, burying the

blade in the trunk of the tree. He left it there, gleaming in the sunshine, while he shrugged out of his jacket and then his shirt.

"Why are you taking your clothes off?" Jaci asked. "It's cold."

"It warms up fast when you start wielding an ax." He yanked the ax from the tree trunk and swung again.

Grace wasn't wielding an ax, but her temperature had just climbed into the danger zone. She'd seen Pierce without his shirt before. He'd been shirtless when he'd shared her bed last night.

But she had never seen him with his muscles rippling the way they were right now. He reeked of masculinity. The fierce hunger for him grew stronger with each swing of the ax.

But did he still want her?

There was only one way to find out.

PIERCE LED DREAMER around the corral with Jaci perched in the saddle and holding on to the reins like a pro.

"Looking good, little lady. Keep this up and you'll be barrel racing soon."

"What's barrel racing?" Jaci asked.

"You race your horse around some barrels. We need to get you to a rodeo," Pierce said. "Maybe we can go see your uncle Tucker compete."

"Okay. Giddyup, Dreamer. We're going too slow,"

she said, obviously having lost interest in barrels and rodeos and an uncle she didn't really know.

But Pierce liked the idea of seeing Tucker again and Riley, too. He'd definitely pencil that on his calendar for spring. Grace would like his brothers and they'd love her on sight.

"I like the way you're handling those reins," Pierce said.

Jaci beamed and tipped her hat, the way she'd seen him do it. Man, had that little charmer stolen his heart.

"Mommy is going to be so surprised that I can ride a horse. She thinks horses are dangerous, but Dreamer's a good horse."

Leslie would be surprised, but definitely not pleased. Leslie had given him a million orders of what to do with Jaci while she was out of the country. Pierce had followed only a few of her rigid rules.

If he'd followed all of them, he'd have been too busy to have fun with Jaci. Besides, this fathering business came a lot more naturally to him than he'd expected. But he had to give Leslie a lot of credit. She'd almost single-handedly raised the most wonderful kid in the world.

Not that he was biased.

He wasn't sure how this split custody arrangement would play out over time, but he knew he loved having Jaci with him.

He loved having Grace there, too. He'd given a lot of thought to the fact that Lacoste was out of prison.

When you got right down to it, he figured this was the best thing that could happen for Grace.

Pierce was working on a plan to put her fears to rest once and for all.

He was still working out the details, but he'd made the right start with a few phone calls. He'd talked to a security expert in San Antonio, to the New Orleans prosecutor who'd tried the case against Tom, to his friend Andy Malone. Know your enemy. That was an important rule on the battlefield. Pierce was working on finding out as much as he could about Tom Lacoste.

Pierce started back to the horse barn.

"One more time, please, Daddy. One more time around the corral. I'm not tired a little bit."

Jaci might get her sentence structure mixed up from time to time, but she always knew what she wanted. Pierce knew what he wanted, too, and she was standing near the corral gate with Esther, both of them cheering Jaci on.

He looked back in their direction. Grace was gone.

GRACE HAD ESTHER'S gentle mare Pansy saddled and standing next to her when Pierce came back into the horse barn with a saddle thrown across his broad shoulder. He looked shocked at first but then broke into his boyish grin that always set her pulse racing.

"What did you do with Dreamer and Jaci?"

"I let Dreamer loose into the pasture. Last time I looked, she was drinking water from one of the tubs of fresh water I filled earlier. Jaci and Esther took the truck back to the house."

He cocked his head to one side and rubbed a spot on his chin. "Who saddled the horse?"

"Me."

"I'm serious."

"So am I. While we're being totally honest, I have one more confession to make."

"Let me guess," he said, obviously picking up on her flirtatious mood. "You got one look at my Christmas tree abilities and realized you can't live without me."

"You did look awfully masculine swinging that ax."

"Aw, shucks, ma'am. That was nothing." He carried the saddle he was holding into the tack room but was back in under a minute. "So what's this big confession?"

"I'm actually an excellent horsewoman. I've been riding since I was ten when my best girlfriend's parents started raising show horses. No cows on their ranch. No chickens. Just horses."

He leaned against the post of Dreamer's stall. "You've been holding out on me. Why?"

"I was afraid that if we started riding together, we might…" She hesitated.

"Like spending time together?"

"That's the gist of it," she admitted.

"So what's changed?"

"I'm no longer afraid of liking you too much."

His brows rose questioningly.

She took a step toward him. "I'm already there."

He crossed the space between them in a heartbeat. She felt the heat generated by their bodies when he took her in his arms. When his lips met hers, she went weak.

One of the horses pawed and snorted. Another started to whinny. She ignored them both. What she couldn't ignore was the loud clattering growl of an engine.

She pulled away reluctantly. "I think we have company."

"Wait right here, I'll shoot them," he joked.

He walked outside. The engine died and she heard voices. When he returned a few minutes later, Buck followed him in.

"Buck's here to clean stalls. I told him we're taking Pansy and Charlie's black stallion, Rocket, for a ride." Pierce turned back to Buck. "We'll be out of your way in a few minutes."

"Take your time," Buck said. "I've got a couple of hours till quitting time and this is the last chore I've got scheduled for today."

The heart-stopping kiss had been interrupted. There was still plenty of time for another. Grace was ready to ride.

PIERCE NEVER FELT freer than he did galloping across wide-open spaces on the back of a majestic horse. Today was no different in that aspect, but riding with

Grace added so many emotional components to the experience, he couldn't concentrate on his horse or the scenery.

She hadn't been kidding. Her experience with horses had been evident from the moment she climbed unassisted atop her mount. Grace took control with confidence and an easy hand on the reins.

But it was a lot more than her horsemanship that had Pierce reeling. He loved the way she looked in the saddle, silky strands of hair flying wildly behind her. Loved her new attitude, as if letting it all out last night had freed her soul.

She kept up with him when she chose to but was comfortable falling behind or speeding ahead when the mood struck. Independent, her own person in spite of what Tom Lacoste had put her through.

She'd managed not only to survive but to take down Tom Lacoste and the rest of his powerful family. Tom had picked the wrong woman to try to control.

Grace might have been the one person in New Orleans who had the spunk and audacity to testify against him and his family. Pierce didn't doubt for a second that Tom would love to rain down revenge on her for that.

If he tried it, he'd meet his match. Pierce had fists that ached to beat Tom's pretty-boy face to mush and the strength and training to do it.

When the horses began to tire, Grace slowed Pansy to a trot. Pierce dropped back to ride at her side.

"I'd forgotten how much I enjoy horseback riding,"

Grace said. "I think I could do this every day of my life and never tire of it."

"Now you are starting to sound like a real cowgirl."

"The ranch life is growing on me," she admitted, "except for getting up at daybreak. I think the livestock should be trained to sleep in."

"I'm sure any rancher who had to leave your bed in the morning would agree with that."

"I don't know. You ran out on me awful early this morning."

"Not by choice. Never think that. You'd had a traumatic night. I didn't want you to think I was taking advantage of you when you were at your most vulnerable."

They slowed the horses to a walk, staying side by side, but not talking. She was so damn easy to be with. He could do most anything every day of his life if he was doing it with her.

"Do you think Charlie was murdered?" Grace asked.

"Where did that come from?"

"I was just thinking. It seems so peaceful out here, but anyone could get on this land if they wanted to. I know it's fenced, but I slipped under the barbwire without too much difficulty."

"And left your car behind," Pierce reminded her. "If you were looking for a quick getaway, walking wouldn't be a great option."

But Grace was right. The fences were made to

keep the livestock in. The gates to the Double K were seldom locked. Besides, even if they were secure, it wouldn't take much for a pickup truck or a four-wheeler to crash through the fence and get access to the ranch unnoticed.

All things to consider when he talked to the security technician tomorrow afternoon. Pierce wasn't expecting Tom to come calling, but on the off chance he did show up at the Double K, Pierce would be ready for him.

Grace pointed off to the east. "Is that a lake?"

"Actually, it's a spring-fed pool that Charlie dammed up so we boys would have a swimming hole. You talk about fun and excitement—try swinging out over the water on a rope and then dropping when you reach the deepest part. That's livin'."

"A little cold for that today," Grace said. "But I'll race you to the pool."

She took off first. The black stallion he was riding could have easily overtaken Pansy, but he stayed a few feet behind for the short ride. The view from the rear was too good to pass up.

Once they'd dismounted, Pierce looped the reins from both horses over a low-hanging laurel branch that allowed them access to a cool drink of water. Even on cold days, horses needed a good deal of water.

Besides, he figured they'd be here awhile. They had a lot to talk about.

Pierce turned and Grace was gone.

"Over here," she called to him and waved from the corner of an old storage shed that looked like it would collapse in the next gust of wind.

"What's this building?" Grace asked. "An outhouse?"

"Cowboys don't need outhouses in the wilds."

"Then why have an old shed in the wilds?"

"You're starting to ask as many questions as Jaci."

"Is that your final answer?"

"Guess not. Back in the day, Charlie built the shed to store feed for the wild animals that came to the pool for water. Mostly he kept corn in there for the deer. But I wouldn't go in there now."

"Do you think it will cave in on top of me?"

"That's a possibility. Even more frightening, it's probably full of spiders, scorpions, wood rats and other creepy, crawling creatures. Might even be a den for an animal."

"Yuck. You should tear it down."

"Good idea. I'll put that on my growing list of things on the Double K that need to be demolished or repaired."

He walked up and pressed his hand against the rough door frame for the front door that had gone missing altogether. Surprisingly, the structure didn't collapse.

He peeked inside to make sure nothing of value had been left there. A gossamer curtain of spiderwebs hung from the ceiling. Using the back of his hand, he brushed them aside to get a better look.

"Do you see any animals?" Grace asked from her spot well away from the crumbling rattrap.

"Spiders." He slapped a giant mosquito against his cheek and stomped on a mean-looking brown spider.

A couple of cane fishing poles with hooks and lines still attached stood in one corner. A pitchfork with a split handle and a rusting ax leaned against the wall and each other on the other side of a ripped burlap bag.

Pierce stepped farther inside and lifted the edge of the bag with the toe of his boot. He stepped back when a scorpion crawled out from under it.

He ground that scorpion into the floor with the toe of his boot, but where there was one, there were probably more.

He walked back outside and brushed the dust from the old shed off his jeans. Hopefully, dust was all he'd collected. If something started crawling up his jeans or neck, he'd shed his clothes fast enough.

"Can we ride up to the bluff again or is that too far away?" Grace asked.

"We can make the ride at a comfortable trot, enjoy the waterfall and still get home in time for supper."

Which gave him another excuse for putting off the dreaded conversation about Lacoste. The news might go down better surrounded by the spectacular scenery.

The wind picked up as they rode toward the rocky ledge. By the time they reached the bluff, the sun was playing hide-and-seek with some dark clouds rolling in from the southwest. Thunder rumbled in the distance.

"Guess this was a bad idea," Grace said. "I should have checked the weather report."

"Wouldn't necessarily have helped. Thunderstorms roll into this area of Texas with little warning, like the one the night you arrived. Hopefully, this one will just blow over."

Grace poked her hands into her jacket pocket and pulled out some wooly gloves.

"It's getting dark and colder," she said. "I think we should just turn around now and go back to the house. I don't relish being caught in a thunderstorm after seeing that show the lightning put on the other night."

That possibility worried Pierce, as well. They turned around without dismounting. Huge raindrops pelted them as they headed back to the ranch. He could see a cloudburst of rain just off in the distance.

"Follow me," he called. He took Rocket to a full gallop and headed for the nearest shelter. By the time they reached it, the temperature had dropped to what felt like freezing and the rain was coming down in sheets.

Pierce helped Grace from the saddle and told her to make a run for the small tin-roofed hay storage barn. He tied both horses to the lean-to attached to the back of the barn and then dashed for cover himself.

Water dripped from the brim of his hat as he stepped inside and out of the storm. He shrugged out of his jacket and hung it on a hook near the door.

He removed his hat to shake the water off, but when he looked up, he forgot the hat, the storm and the temperature.

His insides quaked. His heart slammed against the walls of his chest. A primal need gripped him, so intense it was crippling.

Grace stood in the middle of the barn, her gaze locked with his as she slid the straps of her wet bra down her arms. Without breaking eye contact, she dropped the bra onto the pile of wet clothing at her feet.

Her hands slid inside the waistband of her black lace panties. She peeled them down to her ankles and then kicked them off. They went flying onto the nearest bale of hay.

"You're way behind, Pierce. Do you need help getting out of your wet clothes?"

He nodded and motioned her nearer.

She took off his hat and tossed it. Then her hands went straight to his belt.

Thank you, God, for the rain.

Chapter Fourteen

Grace struggled to unzip Pierce's jeans over the bulge that stretched the denim taut. Slowly, she tucked her hands inside his briefs and slid her fingertips down the full length of his erection and then back up again. When she reached the tip the second time, she caressed his bulge with her right hand, squeezing gently.

Pierce moaned and gripped her shoulders. "Take it slow, baby. I won't last long at this rate."

"Then I may need some help getting you naked."

"Enough said."

She watched in awe as he wiggled out of his jeans and briefs and made quick work of his shirt. His body was magnificent, broad chested with a cluster of dark hair around his nipples and then narrowing until they skimmed his navel.

He was muscular in all the right places. His abdomen looked rock hard. His thighs were perfection in every way. He was like a dessert that made your mouth water but looked too good to eat.

Poor example. Never had her mouth watered for any dessert the way she was growing slick for Pierce now.

While she stood agog, Pierce turned, picked up a pitchfork and made a mattress of loose, sweet-smelling hay. He grabbed a Mexican blanket from a stack near the back of the storage building and spread it over the sweet-smelling hay.

Then he walked over and let his gaze travel from the top of Grace's head to her toes and back up again.

"You're beautiful," he whispered. "Inside and out. And I'm going to go stark raving mad if I have to wait much longer to make love with you. So please tell me this is not a tease."

"I want you, Pierce, the way I've never wanted any man before. I want all of you and I want you now. In my mind and in my heart, this will be my first time to make love."

She would not let the horrors of the past steal any of the joy of making love with Pierce.

He picked her up and carried her to their bed. He kissed her hard, ravaging, claiming her entire mouth with thrusts of his exploring tongue. She melted into the passion of his kisses, into the thrill of Pierce.

His lips trailed her neck past her cleavage, kissing and nibbling on each nipple in turn while his hands caressed and massaged both her breasts. She arched toward him, so aroused her body begged for more.

His kisses moved lower, down her abdomen, sinking into the wet, writhing cradle of her womanhood.

She was weak with the hunger for him. She craved all of him. Deep inside her so that they were one.

He pulled away.

She trembled. "Did I do something wrong?"

"I don't think you could if you tried."

"Then what is it?"

"Protection. Like a damn fool, I didn't bring any. I thought we were only going to the horse barn and corral. I'm guessing you're not taking birth control."

"No, but give me a minute." In the heat of the moment, she'd never given protection a thought. Pierce's concern for her only made her want him more.

Dizzy from interrupted passion, she could barely stand. She managed to stagger the few steps to her wet jeans and pull a condom from her right pocket. She tossed it to Pierce, who caught it with one hand.

"You're amazing," he said. "When did you get this?"

"I found it in the top drawer in my bathroom. I presume it was left by a previous guest."

"Whoever that was, I owe him big-time."

She climbed back into their bed of hay while he pulled on the condom.

"Just so you know, I'm crazy about you, Grace. I've never felt the way I feel about you for any other woman. This is the real deal for me."

"And for me."

And that was enough. She didn't want or need any promises of forever. She needed this moment in time and somehow she'd make the afterglow last forever.

Pierce straddled her and drove his erection deep inside her—over and over again, the rhythm building in intensity until they both erupted in a mind-blowing orgasm.

Pierce had been right to wait. The hay, the sound of rain on the tin roof, even the confusion over the condom—it was all unique and perfect. A night she'd remember and treasure for the rest of her life.

THE RAIN STILL drummed against the tin roof. Pierce would have been content spooning his body against Grace's until morning—or until the wanton desires took over again. But he figured he'd put off the inevitable long enough.

He forced himself to disentangle from her shapely legs and slide off the hay. Unraveled from Grace, an icy chill seeped deep into his bones.

Pierce grabbed two clean blankets, threw one across his bare shoulders and unfolded the other and draped it across Grace's legs.

"I'm not encouraging you to cover any of your magnificent body parts, but just in case you're cold."

She tugged the blanket up to her chin.

He picked up their wet clothes and spread them over the stacks of hay bales so hopefully they'd dry out a little before they had to put them on again.

He did fine until he got to Grace's black panties. His libido jumped right in and he had to turn away from Grace before she noticed his bulge.

"It's still raining," Grace said.

"I know. I like the sound of it on the tin roof."

"So why did you leave me all alone in our love nest?"

"So that I can try to get my brain in gear."

"It's not your brain I'm interested in right now."

"Nor am I. I would love to come back to bed with you and taste every inch of your scrumptious body."

"And the reason you're not?"

"We have to talk."

"You want to talk? This is about Tom, isn't it? You changed your mind about wanting me around your daughter. You don't have to apologize. I told you I should leave."

Grace was trying to sound brave, but Pierce could hear the hurt in her voice. "You know you really should stop trying to read my mind. I'm not that complicated. I say what I mean. I'm here for you and always will be."

"Then what is it and why do you look like you're dreading what comes next?"

"Because you are not going to like what I'm about to tell you."

"You're scaring me."

"I don't mean to, but I don't want to sugarcoat anything, either. I did some investigating this morning. It seems your monster ex is no longer in prison."

She jerked to a sitting position. The blanket fell away, exposing her perfect, perky breasts. She didn't bother to cover them again.

"There must be some mistake. Tom was sentenced

to consecutive life sentences without even a chance of parole for twenty years."

"A judge in Louisiana reversed that."

"Based on what?"

"An illegality in the way the evidence was collected."

Grace stood and made a sarong of her blanket. She paced the room, holding up the ends of the blanket so she didn't trip. "Are you telling me that Tom is back on the streets so that he can start killing again? And some judge ordered that?"

"Unfortunately, yes."

"How long has he been out of prison?"

"A little over a week."

"Then you can bet he's looking for me right now. He won't give up until he finds me and makes me pay. It's the way he operates. The judge's decision just reinforces what I've always known. The Lacostes always win."

"Tom won't win this time, not if he expects to hurt you."

"You still don't get it, Pierce. How could you? You didn't watch him murder his best friend in cold blood. You didn't hear the threats he made to me on a daily basis."

Pierce reached for her hand. She jerked it away.

"It wasn't your grandfather he murdered and you weren't sitting in that courtroom when he shot daggers at me with his cold, murderous eyes and screamed at me that I would pay. If it was the last thing he ever did, he would make me pay. You weren't there, so you can't possibly grasp the evil Tom is capable of."

"I'm sorry. I didn't mean to insinuate that I understand him the way you do. But I have learned a few things about him today."

"That he's rehabilitated. That prison's changed him. You can't change an evil heart, Pierce. And he's evil to the core."

"You're putting words in my mouth again. I had a long talk with my friend Andy Malone, who works for the FBI."

"Don't you think I should have been the first one you talked to about this?"

"Probably, but I knew you'd react like this and I wanted to be able to give you facts and not just nail you to the wall with bad news. Look, you can lash out at me if it makes you feel better, Grace. I can take it. But at least listen to the rest of what I have to say."

"Okay." She took a deep breath and exhaled slowly. "I'm listening."

"I thought there might be a chance the FBI had Tom under some kind of surveillance, so I called Malone. He got back to me. As it turns out, they are tracking him."

"Why?"

"Over twelve million dollars' worth of street drugs went missing at the time the arrest warrants for the Lacoste family members were issued. Neither those drugs nor the money they would have brought in the open market have ever been accounted for."

"And they think Tom will lead them to the drugs or the money?"

"They definitely think he'll go after that before he tries to settle scores with you or anyone else."

"Do they know where Tom is now?"

"Staying with a wealthy friend from the old days in Miami. The friend is supposedly going straight now, but he was a drug runner in his younger days. He and the Lacostes were supposedly friends."

"And they think he's helping Tom reclaim the family losses."

"Or that Tom thinks his friend ended up with the money. Once Tom gets his hands on that, they expect him to skip the country. Gone from the good old USA for good unless they arrest him on new charges regarding that money."

"Who is the friend?"

"A man named Calvin Grange. Have you ever met him?"

"Not that I recall, but the name sounds familiar."

Grace hugged her knees and readjusted her blanket. "That all sounds good, but they're just suppositions, not facts. The FBI has been known to make mistakes."

She was still worried. He understood it, but he hated seeing her have to deal with this all the same. He reached for her hand again and this time she didn't pull away.

"I know this is disturbing, Grace, but I don't want you to do anything rash. I'll do whatever it takes to keep you safe. I promise I will never let Tom Lacoste lay a hand on you again."

"It's not me I'm worried about. It's you and Jaci and Esther." Shudders shook her body and she seemed to dive back into her frustration and fear. "He'll kill you all, Pierce. If he gets a chance, he'll kill you all to get back at me, the same way he did in my nightmare. He murdered all three of you. I saw your bodies and heard him laugh."

She'd seen them all dead in her nightmare. No wonder he'd found her in such a disturbing state.

"It was only a bad dream, Grace. You know it's not real."

"But it could become real. I can't let that happen. You must see that."

He scooted closer and put his arm around her shoulders. "Tom's been out of prison over a week. He's in Miami, not New Orleans and not Texas. He's not likely to ever be in Winding Creek. If he shows up, I'll take care of him. You have to trust me."

"I trust you. But I know what Tom is capable of."

"And it's time you know what I'm capable of. I didn't earn those medals in a Ping-Pong tournament."

"I know that, but we should call Esther. Call her now and make sure she and Jaci are safe."

"I'll call, but there's absolutely no reason to think they're not safe."

He punched in Esther's number. The call didn't go through.

"It won't connect," Pierce explained. "The storm must be interfering with service."

"We have to go back to the house now," Grace said. She started pulling on her wet clothes. "It's almost stopped raining and we can't get much wetter anyway."

It was killing him to see her that frightened. If only he could get his hands on Tom Lacoste. But his biggest worry now was that Grace would take off like a deer in the headlights and end up running scared for the rest of her life.

He couldn't let that happen. He couldn't lose her to her fears of a madman. Pierce's dreams had to be stronger than her nightmares.

His dreams all involved Grace sleeping in his arms every night for the rest of their lives.

THEY RODE HOME in their sticky wet clothes, bundled in blankets that offered little protection against the wind and cold. The only thing going for them was that the rain had given in to a light mist, the worst of the thunderstorm having moved on.

The weather conditions didn't really bother Pierce. He was used to extremes in temperature and challenges to his physical endurance that made this seem like a short hike in the sunshine. It didn't seem to bother the horses, either, now that there was no lightning and thunder to spook them.

Yet knowing that Grace was dealing with an avalanche of fear again was killing Pierce.

"You can dismount at the house," he said. "I'll take the horses back to their stalls once you realize that all is well with Esther and Jaci."

"Thanks."

As they got closer, he could see the Christmas lights on the porch and smell the wood smoke drifting from the chimney. Half the lights inside the house were on, too.

A few minutes later and they had a good view of the Christmas tree through the large family room window, its twinkling lights beckoning them home.

Home. It did feel that way. Jaci and Grace were the main reason for that.

"There's Jaci," Grace called. "See, she's standing next to the tree."

The joyous relief in her voice eased the tension in his neck and shoulders. He hated to admit it, but Grace's fear had been contagious, spreading a bit of her anxiety to him.

The world slid back into a weird kind of normal.

"Whose car is that parked behind your truck?"

Pierce turned to check out the car that he hadn't noticed before. "Probably a neighbor Esther called to come over and see the tree. She's excited about having all of us here for Christmas."

"Jaci is her shiny ornament," Grace said. "You are the gift she needed to help mend her grief."

If that were true, then Grace was the length of shiny ribbon that tied everything together for all of them.

Tom Lacoste? He was the enemy whose tyranni-
cal reign was about to come to an end. Until it did,
Grace would never be able to start putting her fears
and nightmares behind her.

As they approached the porch, Pierce saw the
sheriff's insignia on the door of the car. He seriously
doubted Cavazos had driven out on a stormy night
to wish them a merry Christmas.

Here we go again.

Chapter Fifteen

Grace felt a ripping pain in her chest as she changed into dry clothes. As soon as she'd slipped into a pair of sweats, she hurried back to the family room, where Esther was entertaining the sheriff.

Pierce had already changed into dry jeans and a pullover and was engaging in small talk with the sheriff.

She sat down and joined them, her nerves so rattled her stomach was in knots.

Esther took over from there. "While you guys talk business, I'll help Jaci with her bath."

Jaci marched a brightly painted wise man toward the manger. "I'm not ready for a bath."

"But it's time," Pierce said. "You'll need to get lots of sleep tonight. It's a big day tomorrow."

"Why?"

Her favorite word.

"It's Christmas Eve and you and I have a little shopping to do."

"Tomorrow's Christmas Eve." Jaci jumped up,

leaving the wise man teetering on the edge of the stable. "Santa Claus comes tomorrow night?"

"Yes, he does."

"Then I better mind Grandma Esther."

She eagerly followed Esther out of the room.

Jaci wasn't the only one who'd forgotten that tomorrow was Christmas Eve. Grace hadn't realized it, either. Time had a new meaning since she'd arrived on the ranch.

Pierce crossed a bare foot over his knee. "I hope this visit means you located and arrested Rcid Peterson."

"We've located him."

"Did you get any indication why he decided to shoot up the town?"

"No, and we won't be getting any information from him. His car was found half-submerged in Winding Creek about four miles south of town. Damn car was stuck so deep in the mud we had to have a big-rig tow truck come out from San Antonio to pull it back to dry land."

"Where did you find Reid?" Pierce asked.

"His body was locked inside the trunk."

"He'd been murdered," Grace said. It wasn't a question, but a statement.

"Yep," Cavazos said. "His ankles were bound and his hands were tied behind his back. Not that he was going anywhere. He had a hole so big in his head that half… Well, you get the picture, Miss Addison. No use in painting you the gore."

No use because she'd seen it all before.

"Do you have any idea who killed him or why?" Pierce asked.

"Not yet, but the way he was killed fits the mold of other gang-style killings. It's damn likely this was drug related, too."

That was a Lacoste-style killing in Grace's mind. Her ex-husband may not have committed the act in person, but she was certain he was behind it.

"As it stands, I don't expect to find any correlation between the Winding Creek shooting and Reid Peterson's murder," the sheriff emphasized. "Well, except that drugs were almost certainly involved in both. We don't have any forensics info on the death yet."

Cavazos might not see the correlation, but Grace did. The bullet that went through the window of the Christmas shop had been meant to kill her. It might have been meant to kill Jaci and Esther, as well.

Tom had hired Reid Peterson to do his dirty work. Reid had bungled the task, which meant he'd let Tom down, so he had to die.

It was the Lacoste code.

But how had Tom tracked her down so quickly? The only reasonable explanation was that the man who'd snapped her photo in the library had managed to follow her to this area, possibly right onto the Double K Ranch.

Grace barely heard the rest of the conversation between the sheriff and Pierce. She knew what had to be done and the time to do it was running out fast.

PIERCE STEPPED OUTSIDE with the sheriff as he was leaving. Grace stayed behind. Grace walked over to the Christmas tree, her gaze drawn to the silver slippers ornament.

Jaci's childlike pronouncement echoed in her troubled mind. *The mostest prettiest tree I ever saw.* Grace agreed.

Jaci skipped back into the room in the adorable flannel holiday pajamas Esther had bought for her. Not showing any signs of fatigue, she turned on her electric Santa and started swaying her hips the same way he was.

"C'mon, dance with me, Grace. It's fun."

"You have Santa. You don't need another dancer."

"Yes, I do." Jaci stopped gyrating long enough to grab Grace's hand. "Do it like this."

Jaci provided an exaggerated demonstration and started singing along with Santa's dance music.

This would be Grace's last night at the ranch. She might as well spend it dancing.

She quickly got into the swing of things. They didn't bother to stop dancing when Pierce stepped back inside. If anything, their moves shifted to the wild side.

"Three dancing Santas," Pierce said. "Lucky me." He planted a kiss on Jaci's and Grace's cheeks.

"Dance with us, Daddy. It's easy." She grabbed Pierce's hand.

Grace took his other hand. "Once you let go, it's the easiest thing in the world."

The three of them swayed their hips together. Another moment to add to the memories that would live with her forever.

Esther found them like that. She didn't try dancing with her weak ankle, but she did sing along with them and Santa in what was surely the most out-of-tune version of the song ever heard.

"I hate to break up the fun," Pierce said, "but I think it's past someone's bedtime."

"Not mine," Jaci protested. "I'm not sleepy."

"You better get lots of rest tonight," Esther said. "The next two days are going to be very busy."

"'Cause Santa comes," Jaci squealed. "Will you read me my good-night story, Grace?"

"I'd love to—if that's all right with you, Pierce."

"Works for me. It will give me a chance to pamper Pansy and Rocket. Never let it be said I let horses be rode hard and put away wet."

"What about supper?" Esther asked. "You and Grace must be starving. Jaci and I had a picnic of peanut butter and jelly sandwiches, fruit and a cookie in front of the Christmas tree tonight, but I can warm you two some leftover soup and corn bread."

"Actually, I don't have much of an appetite," Grace said. "Maybe I'll just have toast and a cup of hot tea after I've read Jaci's story."

"Pshaw. That's not enough to keep a bird alive."

"Don't worry about me, either," Pierce said. "I'll rustle up something."

A few minutes later Grace was propped up beside Jaci in her bed.

"What shall we read?" Grace asked.

"Cinderella." Jaci handed her the book.

The tattered edges hinted it had been read many times before.

Grace purposely skipped or changed up a sentence every now and then just to watch how quickly Jaci would correct her. She had every word of the book memorized.

When they got to the last page, Jaci reached over and touched the silver slippers on Cinderella's feet.

"And the prince took Cinderella's slippers and made her go barefoot ever after."

"No," Jaci corrected. "And the prince and Cinderella lived happily ever after."

Grace's eyes grew moist. She reached over, grabbed a tissue from the bedside table and dabbed at her eyes. She was really starting to lose it when a stupid fairy tale's happy-ever-after got to her like that.

"Are you crying?" Jaci asked.

"No, just something in my eye."

"Do you have any little boys or little girls at your house to read to?"

"No, I live alone."

"Why?"

"I'm not married."

"You could marry my daddy. He needs a wife. Then you could be my second mommy."

"I don't know how your daddy would feel about that."

"We could ask him. I have a second grandma now and I'm getting a second daddy soon."

"Do you like this second daddy?"

Jaci nodded enthusiastically. "His name's Dan and he's real nice. He doesn't have horses, but he has a beach house."

"Horses and a beach house. That sounds like a nice life."

"Mommy says she and Daddy will always be my real parents, but you can't have too many people that love you. A lot of people love me. Do you?"

"I definitely love you, Jaci Lawrence."

"I love you, too." Jaci gave her a big hug.

"Now I have to get out of here and let you get some sleep." Grace kissed Jaci on the cheek and tucked her in.

"Your eye's got something in it again," Jaci said.

"Yes, it does." She grabbed another tissue and hurried away before the tears became sobs.

She went back to her room and locked the door behind her. If she spent the night in Pierce's arms, she might never get the strength to do what she had to do.

She packed a few things in her tote bag and large handbag and laid out the clothes she'd change into in the wee hours of the morning. That was it. She could never look back as she drove away from the Double K Ranch for good.

PANSY AND ROCKET were back in their stalls, looking sleek after their brushing and their fill of fresh drinking water. All the horses munched contentedly on the fresh hay Pierce had added to their feeders. He added an extra helping of Charlie's special food mix for Pansy and Rocket. They'd earned it tonight.

What a night it had been. He'd made love with Grace. That ranked right up there with the day he'd seen Jaci for the first time.

From that point on, the night had plunged downhill like a runaway roller coaster. The sheer magic of their lovemaking had been all but buried in the news he'd had to deliver.

And then Grace had gotten the double whammy. It hadn't taken a rocket scientist to read Grace's mind when she was listening to Cavazos. She was convinced the shooting they'd believed was random and the murder of the shooter were both linked to Tom Lacoste.

As much as he wanted to, Pierce couldn't call that far fetched. He'd have to act accordingly. They would need some security at the ranch.

When he'd walked out to the car with Cavazos, he'd questioned the sheriff about the possibility of hiring an off-duty policeman to guard the house for a few days.

Leaving Tom Lacoste out of it for now, Pierce justified the need by saying Esther and Grace had been traumatized by the shooting in town and he wanted them to feel safe while they were coming to grips with it.

Cavazos wasn't surprised. He figured it was mostly

Esther who was worried, since she had the tomfool idea that Charlie had been murdered on the ranch. Nonetheless, he'd said to give him six to seven hours' notice and he could have a reliable, highly competent deputy on duty.

Now Pierce just had to keep Grace on the ranch, so if Tom Lacoste did show up, he could protect her. Basically it all came down to whether she had more trust in Pierce's ability to keep her safe or in Tom Lacoste's determination to get revenge.

His phone vibrated. He checked the caller ID. Andy Malone.

"What's up?"

"It's more what's gone down," Andy said. "Are you with Grace right now?"

"No. I can talk."

"Good, since you might want to break this to her gently."

"That bad, huh?"

"Definitely bad for Calvin Grange but not necessarily for Grace. The bodies of Calvin and his live-in bodyguard were found a few hours ago floating face-down in the lavish swimming pool inside Calvin's Miami estate."

"Guess I'd be pretty safe in assuming this wasn't an accidental drowning."

"Both shot in the head at close range, hands and feet bound and the home safe open and empty."

"Any sign of Tom Lacoste?"

"No, but he's the number one suspect in the murders."

"What does Forensics say about time of death?"

"Possibly as long as two days ago."

Pierce muttered a string of curses. "Then Lacoste wasn't necessarily in Miami this morning when you and I spoke?"

"No. No one saw him leave, but if he escaped with the cash from Calvin's safe, he could be anywhere in the world by now."

"Even Texas," Pierce said.

"That's why I gave you a call the minute I got this update."

"I appreciate that."

"A local FBI agent will be in touch with you tomorrow, but odds are Tom and the money have left the country and he's sunning on a beach in Sicily or Paris."

Pierce never liked to play the odds. "Keep me posted."

"I will," Malone promised. "You do the same. And for the record, if I had to deal with Lacoste, I wouldn't have a worry in the world if you were riding shotgun."

"The problem is convincing Grace of that."

Pierce checked his watch as he broke the connection with Malone. It was ten before nine. He placed a call to Cavazos's private number.

He explained the situation as succinctly as he could. "Can you have an off-duty officer here by daylight tomorrow morning?"

"Yes and a couple of more deputies keeping an eye on the ranch. If Tom Lacoste shows up here to cause trouble, it'll be waiting on him."

"I appreciate that. Have the deputy call when he gets here and I'll meet him by the front gate."

"Consider it done."

What Pierce would love right now was to go back to the house, shower and climb into bed with Grace. Fat chance she'd be in the mood for that after all she'd been slammed with tonight.

He didn't expect to get much, if any, sleep tonight anyway. First watch went to him.

Chapter Sixteen

So this was where the bitch had ended up—on a ranch in Podunk, Texas, with an old, half-crippled woman, a no-class cowboy and a kid.

Tom slowed the Jeep rental vehicle to a crawl to get a better look at the metal gate. Wouldn't take much to break through that.

He wouldn't bother. Reid Peterson had done the legwork for him, mapped out directions to a back gate that was guaranteed to get him inside all that barbwire without anyone noticing.

Then all he'd have to do was wait for the cowboy to leave the house. He'd kill the old woman and kid first so Grace could watch. He might even make her kill one of them. Kill one to save the other. That would tear the heart right out of that two-timing, double-crossing slut.

And then he'd kill the one she thought she'd saved. Sweet, sweet revenge. He'd waited years for this. Eaten prison slop with a bunch of stinking thugs when he should have been eating lobster and steak. Drunk water and weak coffee when he was used to the finest wines. Had to barter for a few lousy smokes.

Worst part of all was having to kowtow to spineless guards that he wouldn't have taken the time to spit on when he'd held the power.

He'd owned the streets of New Orleans. His father and uncles had built the business, but they were growing soft even back then. His younger cousins ignored the code. You couldn't hold the French Quarter much less the Ninth Ward without living up to the code.

The power would have all belonged to Tom by now if he'd killed the sleaze back then. It was too late to go back, but it was not too late to make her rue the day she'd ever turned on him.

You double-cross Tom Lacoste, you pay with your life.

But first he'd put the hurt on her. Put it on her big-time. And then the chartered plane would be waiting on him.

Rio would be great this time of the year.

Chapter Seventeen

Grace opened her eyes and fought the dregs of sleep. Shadows crept about her walls like long-legged witches in the dim gray of predawn.

Reality checked in with a sudden vengeance.

She had to get moving. She threw her legs over the side of the bed and padded to the bathroom.

Move quickly but quietly. Get out while the others sleep.

Grace took care of her bathroom needs including brushing her teeth. That done, she slid her wet toothbrush into its plastic holder and dropped it and the toothpaste into the tote.

In seconds she'd pulled on jeans and a blue sweatshirt. The red boots took a little longer, but she wasn't about to leave them behind.

Not bothering with a hairbrush or makeup, she slid her handbag and tote over her left shoulder and grabbed her parka.

Barely daring to breathe, she eased open the bedroom door. The hinges squeaked. Not loud, but still she hesitated, half expecting Pierce to come rushing down the hallway.

He didn't. She looked back only once as she tiptoed down the hall and tiptoed through the family room.

"Merry Christmas," she whispered as she opened the front door and then closed it quietly behind her.

She was leaving a huge part of herself and most of her heart behind. So much had happened over these past few days.

She'd made a friend in Esther.

She'd let a precocious little girl worm her way into her heart.

She'd fallen in love.

And if she kept thinking like this, she'd never drive out the gate.

Once the door closed behind her, she rushed to her car, opened the unlocked door and tossed her tote and handbag into the passenger seat. She refused to let herself look back at the house as she pushed the key into the ignition.

She turned the key. There was a low growl and then nothing. She tried again. This time there was less of a growl. The engine stayed silent. She tried repeatedly with the same results.

Her frustration swelled to breaking. She beat on the steering wheel with her fists. This wasn't an accident. Pierce hadn't wanted her to leave the ranch and he'd made sure she couldn't.

But this wasn't his decision to make.

She got out of her car and rushed over to Pierce's

truck. She'd drive it to the nearest Greyhound bus stop and get the first bus to anywhere.

The truck doors were locked tight, though she knew he'd left it open and the keys dangling from the ignition when they'd come back from town yesterday.

She walked over to Esther's car but knew she'd find the same. Locked. Pierce was nothing if not thorough—and stubborn.

Pierce thought he could make everything right, but he didn't know Tom Lacoste the way she did.

Grace started to shake. Tears spilled from her eyes and ran down her cheeks. She couldn't drive away, but she couldn't just go back inside, either. Pierce and Esther would be getting up any minute and she refused to let them see her this desperate.

Pierce would take her in his arms and this time he might make her believe he could protect them all from Tom Lacoste.

He'd be wrong.

She stumbled away from the house, paying no attention to where she was going until she realized she was on the long stone path to the horse barn. Riding might be the only thing that could settle her ragged nerves and help her handle the exasperation.

Saddling Pansy did little to ease her anxiety. If anything, the quiet, dark barn was making things worse. She could almost swear someone was watching her from the shadows.

The eerie sensation didn't go away until she'd put distance between her and the horse barn. She took

Pansy to a full gallop, leaving the house, the horse barn and even Pierce far behind her.

She'd never wanted anything in her life more than she wanted to spend Christmas on the Double K Ranch. But every minute she stayed brought them all closer to tragedy.

One way or another, she'd be on her way before dark set in again.

Chapter Eighteen

Amazing how even the best laid plans sometimes changed for the better. This was turning into perfection in every way. The old spirit churned inside Tom. He couldn't return to the life he'd loved, but things were shifting his way.

First, he'd forced Calvin Grange to open his safe, promising all he would take was the twelve million that was actually his. But once he'd shot Calvin and his bodyguard, there was nothing to stop him from taking the twenty-plus million just lying around in Calvin's safe.

And now Grace was out alone at daybreak, walking—or rather riding—right into his hands. He'd been hiding out in the tack room, waiting for enough light to see his way around, when Grace had practically stumbled into the horse barn.

He'd ducked behind stacks of feed and watched her while she'd hefted a heavy saddle from the stand. He could have killed her then, but his fun might have been interrupted by the cowboy.

Killing was far more enjoyable when it was slow and torturous. In Grace's case, that was mandatory.

Tom wasn't afraid of the cowboy, but he'd likely be toting. It would be better to take him one-on-one.

To Tom's surprise, the clueless cowboy hadn't shown and Grace had started her ride alone.

She'd always loved to ride, had begged Tom to buy her a horse when they were first married. He didn't, mainly because he loved watching her beg.

Tom had ridden when he was younger, but he liked things that moved faster, like the Porsche his dad had bought him when he turned sixteen.

A dark brown horse with a mane that looked like it had been splattered with white paint snorted and pawed the ground as if he wanted out of his stall.

Tom checked out the horse's name. He fisted his right hand and shook it at the horse. "You want a piece of this, Sargent? Take me on. Let's see what you got. No? Then let's take a ride."

He went back to the tack room for a halter and reins, not bothering with a bridle or saddle. He wouldn't be riding far. Once he caught up with Grace, the real fun would start.

He wouldn't get to kill the others first for Grace's viewing pleasure, but he'd find plenty of other ways to torture her.

And then he'd kill her.

If you double-cross Tom Lacoste, you pay.

Chapter Nineteen

Pierce climbed in the front seat of the squad car and introduced himself.

The deputy offered his hand. "Kirk Jenkins. Sorry if I kept you waiting."

"You didn't. I couldn't sleep and figured a walk might help clear my mind."

It also gave him a chance to check out the area. He wasn't worried. He had a flashlight in his pocket and a Smith and Wesson on his hip.

He still found it hard to believe a guy who was trying to flee the country with a safeful of cash before he was arrested for murder would be dumb enough to travel to Texas to kill his ex-wife.

But even dumb enemies carried smart bullets.

"Did Sheriff Cavazos tell you why I needed security?"

"We covered it. Is there anything new I should know?"

"No, but I don't want to frighten my daughter. If

she asks why you're here, just tell her you're waiting to see me about some cattle business."

"Right. Any other particulars I should know about?"

"Esther knows about Reid Peterson's murder but doesn't know anything about Tom Lacoste. I'm leaving it up to Grace to tell her what she wants her to know about that, so I'll just inform Esther you're here to provide some extra security."

"Got it."

"Grace is not to leave the ranch without me under any circumstances."

"Looks like somebody's fixin' to head out now," Kirk said. "Car door's already open."

Pierce swore under his breath. He wasn't surprised, but he was irritated that Grace had so little faith in him. She'd no doubt figured out that he'd disabled the engine and was back in her bedroom fuming at him.

If that was the way it had to be to keep her there and safe, then it was the way it had to be.

"C'mon inside," Pierce said as he got out of the squad car. "I'll introduce you to Esther. This is actually her house."

"Is she your aunt?"

"No, but she's like kin, better than most."

"Do you really want to wake her this early?"

"It's Christmas Eve and the sun is peeking over the horizon. Believe me, she'll be up, probably already cooking breakfast. She'll offer you some. Take it. Whatever it is, you'll love it."

Just as he figured, Pierce smelled fresh brewed

coffee and frying bacon the minute they stepped inside. They joined Esther in the kitchen and Pierce did the introductions.

Esther looked Kirk over. "If you're here with bad news, we don't want it," she said. That didn't stop her from filling a couple of mugs with coffee and handing one to Kirk.

"I hired him to give us a little extra security. I thought it might make you and especially Grace feel a bit safer."

"I got a shotgun to make me feel safe and I'll wager I'm as good a shot as the deputy."

"Yes, ma'am," Kirk said. "I believe you. I'm not expecting there to be any shooting today, but if there is, I'd appreciate you leaving it up to me. Gotta earn my pay."

"Does Grace know about this?" Esther asked.

"No. Would you explain Kirk to her when she gets up? I've got to see the animals are taken care of. It's Christmas Eve and we gave Buck the day off, but I won't be gone long."

"You can take a minute to talk to Grace, Pierce Lawrence."

He nodded. He'd rather give her time to cool down over the car trick, but he might as well face her.

He tapped lightly on her door.

No answer.

He knocked again, louder this time.

Still no answer.

He opened the door a crack. "I can explain, Grace."

Still no response. He pushed the door open and stepped inside. The bed was unmade but empty. The bathroom door was open. She wasn't in there, either.

She was gone. If this was a stunt to get back at him, it wasn't funny. Anxiety scratched along his nerve endings. He rushed outside. No sign of her. He called twice.

He raced to his truck, unlocked it and grabbed his rifle. There were muddy hoofprints and boot prints all over the front yard from last night, but there were some new ones, too. He studied them to determine which ones were the most recent. Grace's boot prints rambled but ended up at the path to the horse barn.

Okay. He could calm down. She'd probably taken Pansy for a ride to ease her frustration with him. It made sense.

Still, the anxiety swelled.

His own words to Malone came back to haunt him. Tom Lacoste could be in Texas.

Pierce took off running. It was almost full daylight now. If she was off on Pansy, it would be easy to follow the hoofprints in the wet earth.

He was breathing hard when he reached the horse barn. Pansy was gone, but they couldn't be far. She'd left the door open to her car while he was meeting the deputy at the gate. He walked over and opened Rocket's stall.

That was when he noticed that Sargent's stall was empty. Someone else was on the ranch.

He led Rocket outside and jumped on his back.

There was no time for a saddle. "I'm counting on you, Rocket. Don't let me down. Please don't let me down."

GRACE SLOWED PANSY to a walk and put her hand to her eyes to block the glare of the early-morning sun. She'd been riding for nearly an hour, most of the time mentally drowning in her dilemma.

She'd practically given Pansy free rein. The horse seemed to know where she was going. They'd made some turns, avoided some wooded areas, crossed a creek Grace didn't remember crossing yesterday and taken a rocky climb up several steep hills.

All well and good at the time, but Grace was ready to turn and head back to the house now and nothing looked familiar. She was officially lost.

Pansy stopped to chew on some tall grass at the edge of a clearing.

"No, girl, no picnicking yet. You got me here. Get me back to the horse barn."

Grace squeezed her legs tighter and rocked back and forth in the saddle. Pansy responded, walking forward and finally breaking into a trot. Almost immediately, the area began to look familiar. A cluster of tree stumps. Two twin oaks, both with roots that crawled over the top of the ground in all directions.

And then she spotted the spring-fed pond where they'd seen the deer yesterday. Pansy wasn't stupid. She'd ended up at a watering hole.

Grace dismounted and looped the reins to a branch

the way Pierce had done yesterday. Pansy stepped into the water, lowered her head and drank.

Grace heard what sounded like hoofbeats not too far behind her. It was probably Pierce following her. She spun around, but no one was there. If they were, they were hidden by the thick clump of mesquite off to her left.

If it was Pierce, he wouldn't be hiding from her. Anxiety clutched at her chest. Paranoia or survival instincts? Or were they one and the same when dealing with Tom Lacoste?

No matter how flustered she'd been, it had been stupid to ride off alone without telling anyone where she was going. Pierce would be worried and undoubtedly annoyed that she'd tried to leave without his knowing.

She pulled her phone from the pocket of her parka and punched in Pierce's number.

"Are you calling me, sweetheart? No need. I'm right behind you."

Tom. Fear gripped her, turned her body to stone. She'd always known this day would come. But why now. Dear, God, why now?

"You can at least turn around and look at me, Grace. It's been a long time since you looked into my eyes and told me how much you love me."

Finally, her brain and muscles clicked in. She took off running. She dared not slow down or look back, but she could hear him closing in on her.

Racing uphill, she spotted the old shed where a

thousand spiders and scorpions lived. The kind of place Tom would love. A torture chamber furnished by nature.

Her phone rang and she realized it was still clutched in her hand. Pierce was calling. It had to be Pierce. She punched the talk button without slowing down and stuck the phone to her ear.

She had to warn him Tom was on the ranch. He had to protect Jaci and Esther. He had to protect himself from a madman.

"Tom." She gasped, her lungs fighting for air as she tried to push the words from her mouth. "Tom. Swimming... Spiders..."

Tom's hand closed on her right arm and the phone went flying from her fingers. Something cold and sharp pressed against the spine at the base of her skull.

A knife. He had a knife.

"Is this any way to welcome your husband?"

"*Ex*-husband."

"Is that why you don't seem pleased to see me, Grace?"

He laughed at his own joke, the same maniacal cackle that haunted her nightmares. Years in prison hadn't changed him. He was the same beast he'd always been.

"Let go of me," she ordered.

"You know I can't do that—not before we've had our fun. Take off the jacket," he ordered. "Let me see if you've let your body go to ruin without my money."

"I'm not taking off anything."

She heard the knife split the parka all the way down the back as if it were butter. "I said take off the jacket."

He was crazy. He'd as soon slice her open as the jacket. She let the ripped jacket slide down her arms and fall to the ground.

He forced her to the shed, the knife now pressed between her shoulder blades. It wasn't pricking through the thick sweatshirt but was a constant reminder of how quickly he could slice a jugular vein or any other part of her body he chose.

"You don't want to go into the shed, Tom. There are deadly spiders and scorpions in there. Wasps and hornets and snakes, too."

"Now you're just teasing me with all those promises of fun."

He shoved her inside the shed. A new kind of fear made her blood run cold. A hand-sized hairy tarantula walked across the middle of the dingy shed as if he were the ruler of that terrifying world.

A huge black rat scampered across the dirty floor and disappeared under a shredded burlap bag. And in the right back corner, almost hidden by the shadows, a broken pitchfork leaned against a rusted ax.

She looked away quickly. If Tom noticed them, he'd find a new game to play.

He swatted at the myriad webs that brushed across their faces with every step. A large black spider fell onto the floor. Tom shuddered as he crushed it with his foot.

He was scared. She'd never seen him scared before, but he was scared of spiders and no doubt rats and scorpions, too. A wasp flew around Tom's head.

He swatted at it and jumped backward. The knife slipped from his nervous fingers. Instinctively, she tried to break away again, kicking and throwing punches that never really connected.

Tom grabbed her and slammed her against the wall.

Pain shot through her shoulder. Dizzy and disoriented, she could do nothing to stop him as he retrieved the knife.

Using his right hand, he twisted her left arm behind her back until the pain grew so intense she couldn't fight back the tears.

"Fall to your knees, Grace. Beg me to stop hurting you. Beg and lick my muddy shoes. Beg or I'll break both your arms."

"No."

He twisted more.

"What did you say, sweetheart?"

"I'm through begging, Tom. You'll kill me no matter what I do, so just go ahead and get it over with."

"Don't talk to me like that, you ungrateful bitch. You're the one who ruined things between us. You turned on me. I married you, gave you my name and everything money could buy. And you thanked me by destroying me and my family."

"You got what you deserved."

She needed to keep him talking. As long as he talked, she kept breathing.

"Did you spend all your time in prison obsessing over me, Tom? Did you and the rest of the Lacostes have people searching for me all this time and couldn't find me?"

"No. The others are all wimps. Depressed losers. They gave up. I spent my time planning this moment. I'm the only one with the guts to make you pay."

Keep him talking. He loves boasting about himself.

"Obsessed and yet it took you all these years to find me? That doesn't sound like the powerful Tom I once knew."

"Believe me, you weren't that hard to find. I didn't start looking for you until a few weeks ago when I realized I was getting out of prison."

"I bet you still needed help."

"I hired the right man for the job. He tracked you to Tennessee and then to Texas. Took him no time at all. That's why he's still living."

Tom hadn't been looking for her. No one had been looking for her. She'd lived all those years in hiding, cloaked in fear, when she could have gone on with her life.

She'd lost those years, but she couldn't bear the thought of losing more. Not now. Not when there was so much to live for.

Keep talking. Save yourself.

She inched closer to the ax. "Is that why you killed

Reid Peterson, because he missed when he tried to kill me?"

"No, I killed him for taking shots at you. He was only supposed to provide the details about where you were staying and who you were hanging out with. I've waited too long to let some druggie steal the pleasure from me."

He stepped closer, his body almost pinning her to the wall. This time he pressed the blade of the knife beneath her chin, forcing her to tilt her head back so far she had to struggle to swallow.

"Now I'm not so sure I want to kill you, after all. I might just slice your face into bloody shreds. Dozens of disfiguring scars to help you remember me for the rest of your life. Think your hotshot cowboy would still want you then?"

Tom would do what he said. She knew he would do it. The ultimate, never-ending revenge. She'd rather die.

She spit in his face. "My cowboy is ten times the man you ever were."

He yanked the knife back, preparing to plunge it through her heart. The back of his hand scraped across a rotting beam, knocking a vicious-looking spider from its web and into his hair. The huge spider's jerking legs dangled inside Tom's earlobe.

Tom dropped the knife to swat wildly at his face.

Grace dived for the ax. She lifted it high, poised to swing.

"You won't do it," Tom said. "You know you don't have the guts to swing that ax."

If she didn't kill Tom, he would kill her. She wanted to live.

Tom lunged toward her. She dodged him and swung the ax. The rusted blade sliced all the way through his leg and he went down in a pool of blood.

She turned away, sick at the sight. When she looked at him again, he no longer held the knife. He held a pistol and it was pointed straight at her head.

Even dying, he'd win.

She closed her eyes as the sound of gunfire split through Tom's agonizing screams.

Chapter Twenty

The bullet had hit dead perfect.

Still viewing through his rifle's sight, Pierce watched Grace sway and then crumple to the filthy floor of the bug-infested shed.

He raced through the opening like a charging bull, jumped over Lacoste's body and fell to his knees beside Grace. Heart thundering in his chest, he gathered her in his arms. "I've got you, baby. I've got you and I'm never letting go."

She opened her eyes and stared at him. "Am I dead?"

He put his hand to her heart. "Nowhere close. You just blacked out for a minute. Are you hurt?"

Her body trembled and her expression changed to fear. "Tom is here. He has a gun."

"Tom is dead, Grace. He will never hurt you or anyone else again. The gunshot you heard was mine."

"How? I mean where did you come from? How did you get here?"

"Let's just say we should probably build Rocket a diamond-studded stall with hot and cold running feed."

Finally, Grace looked toward Tom's body lying facedown in his blood. Spiders were already crawling through his raw flesh.

"Tom's dead. He's really dead."

"Died in the same way he dished it out—from a bullet to the brain."

"I chopped off his leg. With the ax."

"Don't sound so horrified. If you hadn't, it would be your body lying there."

"And if you hadn't shot the second you did, I would be dead anyway."

He couldn't even let himself think of how close he'd come to losing her. Relief spilled from his overflowing heart and settled in his soul. Carefully, he picked up Grace, cradled her in his arms and carried her out of the shed and into the sunshine.

Once there, he could see the red marks on her arm and a bloody spot beneath her chin. Fire burned in his belly. "What did that monster do to you?"

"He roughed me up a bit, but that's all. I'm fine, or I will be in a day or two. He did nothing to me that matters now."

"It doesn't look like nothing to me. I'm calling Esther. She can have the deputy come out in my truck. I'll drive you back to the house and he can handle the crime scene."

"Thanks. I might not be quite horse ready yet, but soon. But what about the horses?"

"They can wait." He pulled her into his arms again, gently, so as not to hurt her. "Don't ever scare me like that again, Grace. We're in this together. You trust me. I trust you. That's the way it has to be."

"Got it."

But there was more he had to say. "I love you, Grace. Damn it all, I can't pretend I don't. Timing might be all wrong to tell you, but I can't help it. I'm so crazy in love with you, I thought I would die for a minute back there."

"But you didn't, and the timing is perfect. I love you right back. You and everything about you. I'm sure I always will."

He kissed her and the horrors of the morning slid back into perspective. Grace was alive. She was there. She loved him. Everything else was just another rodeo.

"I'll call the sheriff and let him know he's got a crime scene to deal with out here. There will be questions and explanations to deal with later, but for now I just want to get you home."

"Home for Christmas," Grace murmured. "I love the sound of that."

Chapter Twenty-One

If Grace had ever dreamed of a perfect Christmas morning, it would have been exactly like this one. Esther in her rocking chair, her unwrapped gifts stacked beside her while she delighted in watching everyone else open theirs.

Jaci was on the floor in front of the tree, engrossed in the Cinderella play set from Santa. That must have been what Pierce went shopping for yesterday, though he may have bought that back in Chicago.

Grace had the best spot of all, on the sofa, snuggled close to Pierce and reveling in the warmth, love and laughter that filled the room. A gift she'd craved for six lonely and frightening years.

Jaci took a break from the play set to open her last gift, this one from Esther. She squealed with delight as she pulled out a handmade apron with her name embroidered on it. She put it on over her pajamas and ran over to get Grace to tie it for her.

"I can help Grandma do all the cooking now," Jaci announced.

"Looks like we've opened every present," Pierce said.

"I see one more," Esther said. "Who is that huge present over there by the TV for?"

"Oh, I almost didn't see that one," Pierce teased.

Jaci ran to the package. "It's for you, Grandma. From me and Daddy." She tried to pick it up, but it was much too heavy.

"I declare. What in the world did you buy that big? I'll have to add a room onto the house to have a place to put it."

"I don't think that's going to be a problem." Pierce lifted the box with little effort, carried it over and set it down in front of Esther.

Jaci skipped along beside him. "I can help you unwrap it."

"Thank you, Jaci. I reckon I'm going to need a lot of help."

Jaci tore off the paper.

Esther stared at the display picture splashed across the heavy cardboard. "That's not what's really in the box, is it?"

"It better be," Pierce said. "That's what I paid for."

"It's a porch swing, Grandma," Jaci explained. "You said you liked this one."

"I didn't mean for you to buy it."

Jaci crawled up in Esther's lap. "Do you like it?"

"I love it, but, Pierce, I don't want you spending that kind of money on me. I don't need nothing this fancy. There's no one here to sit in it but me."

"What would you say to having a few more people around here to sit in it?"

Ester leveled her stare at him. "What are you saying, Pierce Lawrence?"

"Just that Jaci and I don't have anywhere we have to be for the next six months. I'm thinking we could stay here. Jaci could register for preschool and ride Dreamer. I could help you get the ranch up and running again."

Esther put her hands over her face, but her pudgy fingers couldn't hide her tears. "Now look what you've gone and done. You've made me cry. I've been praying every day that you'd stay awhile."

"Careful what you pray for," Pierce said. "I may never leave. Ranching seems to be in my blood."

Jaci left Esther and walked over to Pierce. "Is it time yet, Daddy?"

"It's time," he said.

Jaci ran back to the tree, crawled beneath the lowest branch and then wiggled back out with a small silver box with a bright red bow clutched in her hand.

She sashayed over like a prissy peacock and placed the box in Grace's lap. "It's from me and Daddy. But mostly from Daddy 'cause he had to pay for it."

"It's from the both of us," Pierce said. "We're a team."

"You're making me afraid to open it." Grace's hands were shaking as she unwrapped the gift. It looked like a ring box, but she knew that couldn't be. But what if it were?

Was she ready for that? Could she trust her feelings after so many years of blocking them?

Was she ready for the life she'd dreamed of living with a man she loved?

She lifted the lid. Her heart jumped to her throat. Pierce pushed off the sofa and got down on one knee.

"I love you, Grace. I know it happened quickly, but I can't imagine spending my life with anyone but you. I don't expect you to give me an answer today, but I'm asking you to marry me. Marry me and make me the happiest man on earth."

Jaci scooted close to Grace. "And marry me, too. We can ride horses and read stories. And fight the roosters. And dance."

"How could I ever say no to that?" Grace slipped her hands inside Pierce's. "I love you, Pierce Lawrence, more than I ever believed I could love any man. You not only drove away my worst nightmares, you've made my every dream come true.

"I've waited six long years to get my happy-ever-after. I'm ready to start it now."

"Is that a yes?" Pierce asked.

"It's a yes, to both of you." She hugged Jaci to her heart.

Pierce stood, pulled Grace up and into his arms. His kiss was sweet, a promise of a world of love yet to come.

Esther broke down in sobs.

Jaci stood in the middle of the room and held out her hands. "This is the most bestest Christmas ever."

Grace couldn't agree more, but somehow she knew that with a lifetime of living and loving Pierce Lawrence in front of her, the best was yet to come.

Jaci flicked on the power to her Santa. "Okay, everybody. Let's dance."

And dance they did.

* * * * *

COMING NEXT MONTH FROM

◆ HARLEQUIN®

INTRIGUE

Available January 17, 2017

#1689 LAW AND DISORDER
The Finnegan Connection • by Heather Graham
Dakota "Kody" Cameron never expected to be taken hostage in her historic Florida manor, especially not by men disguised as old-time gangsters searching for a fortune hidden somewhere on the grounds. Among them is undercover FBI agent Nick Connolly, who must protect Kody before she recognizes him from their shared past and compromises his cover.

#1690 HOT COMBAT
Ballistic Cowboys • by Elle James
Working for Homeland Security brings John "Ghost" Caspar home to Wyoming, far from the combat he knew as an elite Navy SEAL. Charlie McClain let go of her old flame years ago, and has been raising her daughter and tracking terrorist threats online—until her anonymity is compromised. Now reunited, Ghost will stop at nothing to keep Charlie and her daughter safe.

#1691 TEXAS-SIZED TROUBLE
Cattlemen Crime Club • by Barb Han
The O'Briens and the McCabes have a deep rivalry and get on like fire and gasoline. So when Faith McCabe's secret affair with Ryder O'Brien results in pregnancy, she keeps the baby secret and walks away. But when her half brother goes missing, Faith knows there's only one man she can turn to.

#1692 EAGLE WARRIOR
Apache Protectors: Tribal Thunder • by Jenna Kernan
Turquoise Guardian Ray Strong isn't sure how he's going to protect Morgan Hooke when he can't take her word about missing blood money for a killer her father took down. But when the young mother is targeted by an ecoextremist group, Ray realizes that Morgan may have more than clues to the missing money—she may know the identity of the extremists who paid her father.

#1693 MOUNTAIN WITNESS
Tennessee SWAT • by Lena Diaz
Julie Webb came back to Destiny, Tennessee, to get away from her estranged husband and family after an unspeakable betrayal. And maybe it's destiny that her new neighbor is Chris Downing, a police detective and part-time SWAT officer, because it's going to take all his skills to protect her when darkness from her past resurfaces.

#1694 WILD MONTANA • by Danica Winters
Both Agent Casper Lawrence and park ranger Alexis Finch know how it feels when love goes wrong. But when a grisly murder unveils a dark conspiracy in Glacier National Park, they can't fight their feelings any more than they can see just how deep the investigation will go before the truth comes to light.

YOU CAN FIND MORE INFORMATION ON UPCOMING HARLEQUIN® TITLES, FREE EXCERPTS AND MORE AT WWW.HARLEQUIN.COM.

HICNM0117

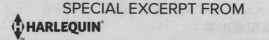
Nick and Kody Cameron had passed briefly, like proverbial ships in the night, but he hadn't had the least problem recognizing her today. He knew her, because they had both paused to stare at one another at the pub.

Instant attraction? Definitely on his part, and he could have sworn on hers, too.

If Dakota Cameron saw his face, if she gave any indication that she knew him, and knew that he was an FBI man...

They'd both be dead.

And it didn't help the situation that she was battle ready—ready to lay down her life for her friends.

Then again, there should have been a way for him to stop this. If it hadn't been for the little boy who had been taken...

Kody Cameron had a ledger opened before her, but she was looking at him. Quizzically.

It seemed as if she suspected she knew him but couldn't figure out from where.

"You're not as crazy as the others," she said softly. "I can sense that about you. But you need to do something to stop this. That treasure he's talking about has been missing for years and years. God knows, maybe it's in the Everglades, swallowed up in a sinkhole. You don't want to be a part of this—I know you don't. And those guys are lethal. They'll hurt someone…kill someone. This is still a death-penalty state, you know. Please, if you would just—"

He found himself walking over to her at the desk and replying in a heated whisper, "Just do what he says and find the damned treasure. Lie if you have to! Find something that will make Dillinger believe that you know where the treasure is. Give him a damned map to find it. He won't think twice about killing people, but he won't kill just for the hell of it. Don't give him a reason."

"You're not one of them. You have to stop this. Get away from them," she said.

She was beautiful, earnest, passionate. He wanted to reassure her. To rip off his mask and tell her that law enforcement was on it all.

But that was impossible, lest they all die quickly.

He had to keep his distance and keep her, the kidnapped child and the others in the house alive.

JUST CAN'T GET ENOUGH?

Join our social communities
and talk to us online.

You will have access to the latest
news on upcoming titles and special
promotions, but most importantly,
you can talk to other fans about your
favorite Harlequin reads.

Harlequin.com/Community

 Facebook.com/HarlequinBooks

 Twitter.com/HarlequinBooks

Pinterest.com/HarlequinBooks

Turn your love of reading into
rewards you'll love with

Harlequin My Rewards

**Join for FREE today at
www.HarlequinMyRewards.com**

Earn **FREE BOOKS** of your choice.

Experience **EXCLUSIVE OFFERS** and contests.

Enjoy **BOOK RECOMMENDATIONS**
selected just for you.

PLUS! Sign up now
and get **500** points
right away!

Earn
FREE
REWARDS
Join
Today!
HarlequinMyRewards.com

MYR16R

THE WORLD IS BETTER WITH

Romance

Harlequin has everything from contemporary, passionate and heartwarming to suspenseful and inspirational stories.

Whatever your mood, we have a romance just for you!